FS

NIGHT OF THE COMANCHE MOON

A Western Story

NIGHT OF THE COMANCHE MOON

A Western Story

by T. T. FLYNN

Five Star Western
Thorndike, Maine

Copyright © 1995 by Thomas B. Flynn, M.D.

A Five Star Western published in conjunction with Golden West Literary Agency.

August 1995

First Edition

Five Star Standard Print Western Series.

The text of this edition is unabridged.

Set in 13 pt. News Plantin.

Printed in the United States on permanent paper.

Library of Congress Cataloging in Publication Data

Flynn, T. T.
  Night of the Comanche moon : a western story / T.T. Flynn.
      p.   cm.
  ISBN 0-7862-0508-3 (hc)
  1. Comanche Indians — Fiction. 2. Kiowa Indians — Fiction.
I. Title.
PS3556.L93N5 1995
813'.54—dc20   95-9437
                                                      CIP

NIGHT OF THE COMANCHE MOON

A Western Story

Chapter One

What did a girl on the wild New Mexico frontier —
an English girl not much past twenty — do when her
brother had vanished? A young man, smiling and vital,
whom she had kissed with affection and watched ride
off with a last cheery backward wave, and high plans
and hopes? Whom she had watched out of sight into the
immensity of distance and time that was called New Mexico Territory?

And what did a man do — a fighting war chief of the
Quahada Comanches — when a son disappeared, probably
killed, possibly wounded and hiding, waterless, hungry,
helpless. . . . Possibly even a prisoner on that great hacienda south of the Bravo River, in Old Mexico?

On an afternoon of brilliant sunlight, Ann Carruthers
made her decision within minutes after the spring wagon
returned from another trip into town, bringing supplies
and the latest mail.

Ann carried the bundle of newspapers, magazines, and
letters into the new massive-walled adobe house and tried
not to hurry. Polinski, the amiable bow-legged wagon
driver and several other ranch hands, including Pete
Wilcox, the foreman, were watching her closely.

Their thoughts undoubtedly matched her thoughts.
When was Geoffrey Carruthers returning to this immense
ranch he should be managing day by day now?

A competent foreman with authority could run any ranch after a fashion. A young woman, part-owner, could make more or less trivial decisions, it was believed. But a new ranch, a huge ranch, the foundation of an empire of cattle and land which would follow, needed a firm man-owner to make irrevocable decisions day by day.

In the long, low-ceilinged living room where peeled overhead logs held up the flat, dirt-covered roof, and bold-patterned Navajo rugs and softer throw blankets brightened the cool quiet, Ann impatiently pushed newspapers and magazines aside on the table she was using and untied the packet of letters. She was not a tall girl. New Mexico sunlight had darkened the rosier bloom of English fogs and oft-times gloomy winters. The narrow leather belt and hand-hammered silver conchos around the top of her brown linen skirt encircled waist and hips that were still small and wiry. Her hair, brown with hints of red-gold in the sunlight, was coiled and pinned close to her head today, and she was frowning as she riffled through the mail.

Many of the letters were off the ocean mails from Great Britain and the Continent. And — again — no word at all from Geoffrey. Ann walked restlessly to one of the deep-embrasured windows in the thick, mud-plastered, whitewashed adobe wall, and looked out across the front portal into the vastness of distance that was this empty, still savage land of New Mexico.

She hadn't, Ann admitted to herself, really expected a letter from Geoffrey today. Her inner dread, which had been a tightening knot for weeks now, had bloomed into a flower of fear. A red flower of shadowy fear, and growing certainty that something disastrous had happened to Geoffrey. For days she had planned.

Now Ann walked back through the house to the room

at the rear corner which was the ranch office. Putting the office here had been her suggestion. It could be entered from the house. Strangers and ranch hands stepped into the office from the outside, transacted their business, and went outside again without invading the privacy of the inner house.

Like everything else on the new ranch, this office still had a little-used, raw look. The roll top desk at the right of the south window was new and gleaming with varnish. The three straight-backed wooden chairs were new. The swivel desk chair upholstered in black hide was obviously new. Gun rack and shelves on the wall had a new, little-used look. And more than once lately Ann had been grateful for this room which kept the rest of the house private. She opened the back door now and called to Pete Wilcox, the foreman.

He came immediately from the loaded spring wagon, a lanky man taller than average with the narrow hips, wider shoulders, and lean torso which seemed universal among these men who were in the saddle more often than afoot.

Wilcox's spare face was not unhandsome, but his infrequent smiles were surface grimaces over a sober lack of humor. He was a serious man who could be goaded into anger. Now the slanting heels of his boots struck the hard, dry ground as if single-minded purpose propelled the man toward the office steps. Ann had noted that also about Wilcox. The man seemed to have an inner, driving energy about everything he did.

Wilcox caught off the flat-brimmed, flat-crowned black hat. His hair was a dark, rumpled mop beginning to streak lightly with gray. He paused at the bottom of the three wooden steps reaching up to the doorway where Ann stood. The cool blankness of his gaze touched her face and waited.

"I've mentioned that it might be necessary that I leave the ranch for a time," Ann said with her own cool calmness.

Wilcox nodded without speaking.

"If I leave early tomorrow," Ann suggested, "can you carry on here without trouble?"

Too late, she realized how foolish it sounded. The leather loops on Wilcox's gunbelt were fat with bright brass cartridges. The wooden-handled gun in his holster had an efficient look. Bandits, Indians, explosive violence were things one lived with in this too often lawless wilderness. She had heard hints that Wilcox's temper made him a dangerous man in trouble. Was there now the slightest shading of contempt in his glance?

At least his even gaze showed no trace of a smile at her rather foolish question. The cool eyes merely rested on her face.

"How long, ma'am, will you be gone?"

"I haven't decided."

Wilcox put one booted, dusty foot on the bottom step and contemplated his hat.

"Be a help if I knew when Mr. Carruthers'd be back."

The blank eyes jumped from the hat to her face again. Fast. Searching now.

"Geoffrey isn't certain when he'll be back," Ann said casually.

"You've heard from him lately then?" Wilcox asked equally casually.

"The mails haven't stopped," Ann evaded coolly. "I'll leave in the morning for Las Vegas and Santa Fe."

"The buggy'll be ready, ma'am."

When Ann turned back into the house to pack for her journey, she would not have believed — even from Geof-

10

frey — that from this decision her life and future merged with wild Comanche Indians whom she had never seen. One Indian in particular. . . .

He was a squat, bandy-legged Quahada Comanche, wearing old skin leggins, a greasy, too-large skin shirt, and a greasier blue cloth headband. He had carried a round buffalo-hide shield, a lance, a single-shot Remington rifle and a buckskin pouch of cartridges. Now he had nothing but the hide-sheathed knife at his hip, the quirt tied to his right wrist, the foam-smeared, near-staggering horse under him.

His left arm flapped limply. Shoulder and sleeve of the skin jacket were dark and stiff with crusted blood. He had not eaten in sixty-three hours — if he had been a man to count hours, which he was not. Water had not passed his mouth in fourteen hours, while blood seeped, seeped from the bullet-smashed arm.

He was a dying man on a dying horse — the third horse, which now was collapsing under him. He had ridden furiously through most of a night and a day, a second night, and this day. Now, in the late afternoon, the world was a blaze of heat and masses of dusty *granjeno* scrub. The unshod hooves kicked dust from the dry earth and drier grass and weeds. The dust hung yellow, lifeless behind them. There was no breeze to put even a searing stir of life into the quiet, oven-shimmer of the afternoon.

The Comanche was riding toward the curious, bread-loaf butte which seemed to crouch and sway and slowly shiver in the glassy waves of heat. Beyond the butte a thin, dark line of cottonwood and salt cedars marked moisture. The ramal ends and the wrist quirt slashed weakly as one, for he had only one hand, one arm to use.

11

The slashes of the rein ends and quirt were not hard enough to change the even slog of the wavering horse. Probably would not have changed the slowing pace if the tough hide had been cut to blood. Bone, flesh, and heart could give only so much. No more.

But the horse still moved on. The rider still burred to the drying salt sweat and foam on the bare back. The quivering butte drew nearer, enlarging, becoming more solid. The salt cedar tops on beyond became full gray-green. Leaves became visible on the cottonwoods — and at their base a sudden ragged burst of movement lifted dust, and became miniature shapes of racing horses and riders.

Eight of them carrying rifles and carbines, stringing out at first, bunching up and coming on at an easier run, swirling finally around the lone, advancing rider like brown-hued, gaudily painted leaves caught in an eddy of heated air.

They were younger men, well-fed and watered, astride fresh horses. Shrill calls and greetings died away before the glazing impassivity of the older man and the unsteady advance of his drooping horse. He had straightened before the first riders reached him.

His back straight now, the useless arm flopping slackly in its blood-crusted sleeve, eyes ignoring the younger men, he rode down a last slant to the greener trees and a thin run of water in a sandy channel. Here were no gabbling squaws, shrilling children, barking dogs. No tee-pees and clutter of a home village. Some thirty men were in sight, younger and older. A horse herd cropped tufted grass along the run of water. Two cook fires smoldered and gave off lean plumes of gray smoke.

This was a war camp, stripped of all excess equipment for the incredible riding done by the raiding Comanches in the days and nights of the full moon. It was one small band of many now scouring the South Plains and probing on south to small ranchos and larger haciendas in Chihuahua as the moon waxed to full brightness — the dreaded Comanche Moon. On all the Texas frontier, and farther south into Mexico, apprehension increased as the moon bloomed full. Some called it the Kiowa Moon, for the fierce treacherous Kiowas rode also under the full moon, often with the Comanches, who tolerated them.

The man who walked out from the nearest cook fire was not the tallest man in sight — but he had the broadest chest. Powerful legs were straight, neck was thick, nose was bold. Men gathered behind him as the lone rider came up and yanked the blowing, quivering horse to a halt and slipped off. He reeled, and started to fall on buckling legs.

Two men jumped forward, caught him, heaved him upright, held him. His words came croaking thickly in the clicking, mouthing Comanche tongue.

". . . to Juan Tomás, grief I bring. . . ."

The lighter-hued features of Juan Tomás hardened, as if he knew what was coming. He gestured to men behind him, without looking around.

"Water. . . ."

An old dented army canteen was already waiting. Thrust at the lone rider's mouth, it slopped water out of the mouth corners, off the dusty chin, over the greasy shirt. He shook off helping hands, braced moccasined feet, sucked gasping breath for a new effort, and said: "The Yellow Hairs of the great rancho have killed Speaking Wolf! They were hiding as we caught horses . . . their guns were many. . . ."

"Juanito . . . ?"

"His horse dropped. I was a man of one arm. When

13

I looked back, I was alone. At the Dirty Spring and Coyote Pool there was no sign of Juanito. I have come to tell you who has taken your son. . . ."

"You have told me."

Juan Tomás was still impassive. The two braids of his hair were rusty brown. Red rags were woven into the ends. Hanging around his neck by a thin brass chain, resting on his wide, bare, painted chest, was a round mirror framed in brass that caught the westing sun in a glinting flash as he moved. He stood for a long minute, thinking, ignoring the man they were supporting in front of him.

"I know the Yellow Hairs," he said, finally. "Now they will know Juan Tomás. Their women will be Comanche slave women for any men to have. Their scalps will dry in the sun before our lodges. Here we wait now, until all who will call me chief are ready to ride. There will be rich loot for all on this great rancho. . . ."

It was on the two huge water wheels of the Hacienda of Our Lady of Sorrows, in Chihuahua, that John Hardisty came to know that unending labor would not break him as it broke many men sent to the water wheels. Such stubbornness was, first, a matter of cording muscles which grew stronger with time. But it was also a greater matter of spirit.

Some men refused to break when aching bones and exhausted bodies cried for the blessed relief which waited close under their dripping feet and jingling chains. Those who weakened or broke — and jumped off or fell off — plunged into muddy water deeper than a tall man and his up-thrust arms and leg irons, wrist irons, and chains anchored them to the bottom until the languid guards hauled them up.

14

A rule of the hacienda seldom varied: if a man cared to live, the price was unending labor on the two huge, dripping, groaning wheels which lifted water from the little man-made lagoon to the higher, pancake-flat grape and vegetable fields of the vast hacienda. Hired labor or peon workers would not have lasted. So Indian slaves and prisoners kept the great wheels turning. All that, Hardisty tried to make plain to the new one — the young Comanche whose fresh chains clink-clanked softly and whose movements on the water wheel treads were leaden and mechanical.

They had brought him in early one night — what was left of him after beatings and brutalities on the trail. His chains had been riveted on. At dawn he had been put on the west wheel. Put at Hardisty's right, where the dull peon from the Vaca Fria country to the south had met his doom for staggering pulque-drunk against the carriage wheel of a matron of the hacienda. That peon had lacked imagination, inner depths, strengths. Hardisty had sensed the end coming.

Chapter Two

He had tried to talk hope into the man — at least talk needed strength and spirit — and, even while he had tried, had known he was failing. It was not a good thing watching a man — a human being — erode and die inside by bits and pieces. Body and soul, that peon had belonged to Don Alfredo Correon de Leon y Delgado, as Big Luis, the head guard, also belonged. Never having seen a soul, Big Luis was not concerned with such things. But he had the coiled whip cut from a bull buffalo hide. He and his men had the fierce dogs — and behind Big Luis and above him, far above him — was Don Alfredo Delgado than whom there was no greater, save God Himself. In all practical matters, it was Don Alfredo who was close and visible day by day.

Some of that Hardisty tried to tell the new man, the young Comanche whose bare feet listlessly trod the same wet wheel planks which Hardisty's callused feet had helped wear smooth. The talk was in Spanish, which Hardisty knew well by now. Nothing else was spoken around the water wheels, or on all the great hacienda, save in the huge, sprawling, many-patioed house where guests from the wide world delighted in the benign, witty, near-regal hospitality of the de Leon y Delgado family.

"Easy, *amigo*," Hardisty advised the new man.

He had guessed rightly that the young Comanche knew

some Spanish. After a moment, he sullenly returned, "Juanito has no *amigos* — no friends."

A slight smile lighted Hardisty's heavily tanned face, slashed above the eyes by bleached tufts of untended brows.

"Juanito — Little John," he said. A flick of his eyes took in the narrow hips, wide shoulders, high, dark-hued cheekbones almost level with Hardisty's own gaunt cheeks. "Not so little a man," Hardisty said.

The smoldering look he got back offered no friendliness, expected no kindness from any of the three near-naked creatures on the dripping treads of the ponderous, slow-moving water wheel. This man wanted nothing from Hardisty, from Carruthers, the Englishman, or from the wild Irishman named O'Meara, over at the other end of the treads.

"Chief's son . . . me . . . Juanito, son of Juan," he spat sullenly, proudly at Hardisty.

Another one, came Hardisty's regretful thought. Another one tearing himself apart inside already, like O'Meara, the really wild Irishman, whose helpless rage at captivity was sapping reserves which O'Meara desperately needed.

"A chief's son?" Hardisty repeated in Spanish, not smiling now. And aloud, to himself in English, as he often did to help sanity, he said, "Not good. You'd better not admit chief's blood."

The young Comanche's head turned quickly, black eyes burning at him, and Hardisty guessed aloud, "He understands Anglo talk, too. He's been around Americans somewhere."

Then memory stabbed, puckering lips in a soft, amazed whistle.

"Juan — John," Hardisty said. "Chief Juan Tomás. . . ."

17

A blaze of resentful understanding flared in the black eyes watching him.

Juan Tomás was the Comanche war chief and notorious raider — and this proud, surly young buck of twenty-three or -four, at a guess, must be the son, probably the oldest son and the favorite of Juan Tomás. The mother of Juan Tomás, so rumor of a thousand miles of ravaged frontier had it, had been a beauty, captured from a California-bound immigrant wagon, and really cherished by the man who took her to wife. It was said he had been reared half-white, even in his thinking. And at least one of his wives was a captured white woman, taken to blanket as a full-right wife, instead of a miserable slave-concubine, scorned and beaten. This Juanito — this Little John — must be the son of that woman.

The dark-hued skin, Hardisty saw now, was darkened more by sun than by blood inheritance. The dirty black hair, critically-eyed, was really a lustrous brown-black. The high cheekbones were not full Indian-broad. Nostrils pinched thin at the base. The mouth was not very full-lipped. This young Comanche warrior looked more Anglo-American than Indian when surveyed closely. But his mind — how much of his mind thought only Co-manche?

"Juanito Tomás," Hardisty said under his breath in English. Another hostile look from the young Comanche met his inquiry, "Do they know on the hacienda who you are?"

O'Meara, standing behind the Englishman on the slow-descending foot planks which moved endlessly as the big wheel turned, heard it and called over in angry mockery.

"Faith! Does he know what he is now?"

"Watch it, O'Meara," Hardisty warned sharply.

Losing control never helped. It merely amused the

18

guards. If annoying enough, it could earn whip welts on a man's back. But O'Meara's temper had burst control again.

"Tell 'im he's no better'n a dog now, like us! Tell 'im, Hardisty, you scut, preachin' calm even when they're peelin' your back with a whip! You — Indian! — see the dogs on the bank over there? They're sizin' you up as one of them! Look around! You see a real man anywhere?"

Big Luis, the head guard, was hunkered against the wall of the prisoners' hut, grinning at O'Meara. Big Luis could not understand the Irishman's bawling brogue, but he enjoyed such outbursts. They broke the monotony. They titillated the sadistic edges of the man's dull mind. Sometimes they stirred him enough to strut closer and use the whip, cursing in Spanish.

The young Comanche glanced around, once more showing that he understood O'Meara, also. He had gazed with trapped defiance when they brought him out of the windowless prisoners' hut, and had obviously been puzzled at what he saw.

In truth, there was not much to see. Several low adobe huts for prisoners and guards, and the cook hut for them all. The hand-dug lagoon and placid ditch of water running along the base of the thirty-foot bluff. Merely one more irrigation ditch in arid country, this one fed by a small stream snaking out of the foothills miles away. The bluff curved around on three sides, cutting off all sight in those directions.

Set on the inner bank of the little lagoon, the two huge water wheels rose higher than the bluff — and, as they turned, spilled water into plank races overhead, from which it ran into shallow ditches which irrigated those higher, richly fertile fields of the hacienda. With some changes, oxen, mules or horses could have turned the wheels. But livestock were wealth. Peons, slaves, prisoners had always been plentiful on such an immense hacienda. Labor on the wheels solved many problems — and spread a silent aura of terror among all of evil intent, even far beyond the hacienda. And from the first, prisoners had meant leg and wrist irons, chains, guards, guns, whips, dogs.

Prisoners ate — so why should they not labor for their food as the good God intended? Custom fitted everything into the long, slow years — slaves, prisoners, the huge cumbersome water wheels — and reckless men like the dark-browed, furious O'Meara, who was swearing now in Spanish, giving his vitriolic opinion of the de Leon y Delgados and, also, his raging opinion of Big Luis and the man's ancestors. O'Meara had a richly endowed tongue.

"Shut it off!" Hardisty called roughly across to the Irishman. "The whip's already at you."

"Whip!" jeered O'Meara. He had not bothered to look around and now he did not look. "Never a whip stopped a man from the truth! Dogs — all of us! An' that Big Luis, the scruffiest dog of all!"

The guard had come off his haunches, snatching up his coiled whip, lumbering in flat-footed rage toward the wheel where O'Meara's lurid shouts bounced off the eroded bluff sides, sounding even louder in the enclosed space around the small lagoon.

"¡Perro — dog!" yelled Big Luis with his usual lack of imagination. "¡Cabrón! I, Luis Gonzalez, show you!"

The lash laid a red stripe on O'Meara's leathery back. O'Meara's laugh was jeering.

"¡Cabrón!" he said. "Who's home in your bed now, fat feeder of sons who lie when they call you father

". . . and all know it!"

A second and third welt sprang crimson across O'Meara's back as rage drove Big Luis past reason. And with a shattering suddenness the blast of a hand-gun crashing through the uproar made even Hardisty instinctively hunch shoulders.

His glance toward O'Meara half-expected the bawling Irishman to be wilting off the wheel treads. But O'Meara, startled into silence, was also staring around. Big Luis had lowered the whip and wheeled to fawn if the shot signaled censure from Don Alfredo. Even prisoners had their value for labor.

Two men were riding into the cul-de-sac on wiry mustangs. Saddles were deep, with carbine boots and large leather saddlebags. Stirrups were long with *tapaderos*. Hats were wide-brimmed, high-crowned straw. And each man wore a yellow, spotted calfskin vest, hair out — the distinguishing sign of the Yellow Hairs — the armed, mounted guards of the hacienda. They were picked men, favored but disciplined. In reality, the Yellow Hairs were the small, private army of the Hacienda of Our Lady of Sorrows.

The first Yellow Hair hauled in his horse, gestured impatiently with the long-barreled-hand gun he'd fired, and ordered shortly, "Put away the tickler, Luis. *No mas* — no more — until it is allowed again."

Big Luis coiled his whip in surly compliance. "Who keeps these dogs quiet and working without a whip?"

"Is that one on the end there the Comanche they brought in?"

"Oh, *si*." Big Luis spat. "He is one crawling Indian, I think, when I have him for a little time."

The first Yellow Hair was short and wiry like his mustang, part Mexican-Indian himself by his looks, stiff-strutting in movement as he shoved the gun back in its holster, and dismounted and dropped reins. He unhooked a small strap-hung *olla* from a ramada pole of the guard shack, tilted the long neck, and poured a stream, swallowing noisily and greedily. With a deep breath and grunt of relief, he handed the small earthen jug to his companion who had also dismounted.

A dusty hand swiped his mouth and black mustache before he said, "One dead Comanche. This one brought in alive. And one escaped with news that the Hacienda of Our Lady is not good hunting for such cursed coyotes."

"Comanches killed my grandfather," said Big Luis. "And there was a daughter of my brother. . . ." He spat eloquently. "This one will beg to die."

"That," said the first Yellow Hair briskly, "is not an affair of mine. Which one is the Englishman, *Car-rrrutherrrrs?*" In Spanish he rolled each r in fluid mockery of the name.

Carruthers, at Hardisty's left, seldom had much to say. He was a lean young man with sandy hair, a spattering of freckles, and a medium build. He was a man with his own depths and resources, and a quiet air of waiting, overlaid at times with melancholia which only Hardisty understood. He was the only man the Englishman had talked to with any frankness since being put on the wheels.

Carruthers had ignored the Irishman's frantic outburst. He had even appeared not to notice the overlap of the whip lash stinging his side, also. The gunshot had brought the Englishman's glance around only briefly. The talk which followed had not interested him. But when his name rolled out mockingly, he looked around again, replying in good Castilian Spanish, obviously university-learned and still untainted by the common Indian-Spanish which had assaulted his ears in past weeks.

22

"I am Geoffrey Carruthers — what is it?"

Even half-naked, sun-scorched, whip welts livid on his back, the man gained in dignity and stature with the precise reply.

Meanwhile, the two huge water wheels were ponderously turning, turning — and, as long as the foot treads came down, the four men on each wheel stepped up in unison to the next descending tread: up, up, step up, step up. It was a way of life which became automatic. No matter what a man was thinking, doing, or saying otherwise, legs and body were stepping up slowly and rhythmically, always keeping the huge, creaking, dripping wheel turning, turning. By their own choice today, the Irishman, the Englishman and Hardisty were on the same wheel. What did it matter, even to Big Luis? Some days they were separated, some days they were together like this on the same wheel.

"*Carrrrutherrrrs,*" the first Yellow Hair said, rolling the name out again. "So?" He pushed back the dirty, high-crowned sombrero and cocked his head. A sly grin twisted his mouth as he eyed the rough, bleached beard stubble on the young Englishman's face.

"The lady," he said, "who looks for Carruthers would hold her nose and run from one like you."

"What lady?" Sudden rising thickness filled Carruthers's demand.

"*¡Aie, de mi!*" The hacienda guard was snickering in his throat. "So pale, that lady. And lovely and sorrowful. Even Capitán Sanchez had the wet, admiring eye as he told her that the *patrón* would know everything." The snicker grew stronger in the guard's words. "And then, behind his hand, Sanchez ordered us to take this man, *Carrrrutherrrrs,* off the wheels quickly."

"To see her?"

"¿Quien sabe?"

For a long moment, Carruthers seemed to freeze as he stared over at the guard's sly grin. The wet foot tread carried him down toward the roiling water as he forgot to step up. A groan of pure anguish burst from him.

"Dear God! Ann, too! Here! And helpless on this hacienda!"

On the jolting, dusty Barlow & Sanderson stage from Las Vegas to Santa Fe, Ann had reread, more leisurely, the letters from home. Aunt Agatha was still gratefully surprised that nephew and niece had not been pin-cushion-stuck with Indian arrows, bloodily scalped and/or tortured. And, in Ann's case, had not yet suffered that further fate worse than death at the hands of bestial savages or desperadoes.

Enough solid truth lay behind such fears to bring only the smallest, wry smile when Ann read such concern from far-away Sussex, where the family roots thrust back into the centuries and, naturally, was still "home." This wild, empty Territory of New Mexico was merely a place where she and Geoffrey had happened to come. They might equally well have gone to India. Or up-country from Singapore. Or to South Africa, Canada, China. The younger men often went out to such far places. The girls, of course, did not, unless they were marrying men who were going.

Ann had been somewhat of a spot on the family tree. An exception, rather different from the ladies of the last several generations. They had been lovely ladies. Perfect ladies. As a small girl, Ann had wished she could have been Sir Walter Raleigh, or Magellan, even if it meant shifting over to the Portuguese side. Geoffrey, six years older, had understood perfectly. So she had planned with Geoffrey about this, both of them deciding on New Mexico because a school friend of Geoffrey's was already there. That the friend had been shot three times through the chest, murdered in seconds by a drunken outlaw who objected to his British way of speaking, and they had missed the funeral by a scant week, had not been enough to change their plans.

There had been money enough to purchase the Vuelta Grant from Simon Roddan, a man of substance and power in the Territory. Enough money from the family and friends of the family to start the cattle empire which Geoffrey had decided they would have. The hastily erected adobe house and outbuildings, the corrals, horses and cattle, the new ranch crew, were only the beginning. The important thing, Geoffrey had reminded with increasing enthusiasm, was the land to expand on — streams, springs, timber, water-holes, grass — and they had all of that on the Vuelta Grant. It was luck. The best of fortune. Nothing now could hold them back.

Then Geoffrey had made his trip away from the huge new ranch. He should have been gone at the most only two or three weeks. Not months.

First he had visited Santa Fe to dispose of many items of ranch business. South then to the smaller village of Albuquerque. Finally, still further south to the town of Socorro, the seat of a county which was, Ann had heard, one of the largest in all the West. The last surprising word from Geoffrey had been mailed at La Mesilla, far south in the Valley of the Rio Grande, near Paso del Norte, in Old Mexico. It had been a brief note, which Ann now carried in her reticule.

Santa Fe was a seething town. Two long wagon trains had arrived scant hours before the stage from Las Vegas raced down the last steep grade and rumbled through

25

narrow, sandy streets. The plaza and streets leading off it were choked with ponderous, canvas-topped freight wagons, with long spans of horses and mules, yokes of oxen, and noisy, milling people. Dusk was already drawing blue-black shadows under the tall plaza trees. The hotel on the southeast corner of the plaza where the stagecoach deposited her seemed as crowded and uproarious inside as the plaza itself.

The clerk had a bald head, a moon face, sad eyes, and a regretful voice when he said that all the hotel rooms were taken.

"Might try across the street," he suggested, without conviction. "Likely they're filled, too — but you c'n try." Ann's distressed annoyance put a bit more concern into his manner. "Might be you know someone in town who'd take you in, ma'am."

"I only know Judge Bassett at the bank. In a business way."

The clerk's manner instantly, subtly altered. "Judge Bassett? Well, now. . . ." He stepped quickly out from behind the counter. "A moment, ma'am; wait here, please."

He was back quickly, followed by the stocky, white-thatched figure of Judge Colin Bassett, who was not a judge now but had been one. The judge was beaming with gallant recognition.

"Miss Carruthers!" He ducked his white thatch over her hand. "So you're the lovely young lady in danger of being put out on the street?"

Behind his counter again, the moon-faced clerk looked increasingly uncomfortable. "Wasn't that bad, Judge. Something could've been fixed up. I was studying on it while I went for you."

But not, Ann thought cynically, before you heard Judge

Bassett's name.

The judge was saying, "The town is full of friends aching for my company tonight. My room here in the hotel is at your service, Miss Carruthers. And if you'll honor an old and lonesome widower by sharing dinner with him after you've had a chance to . . . to rest?"

"The best I had hoped for, Judge Bassett, was to talk with you in the morning at the bank."

"And now," the judge said, chuckling, "my good fortune lets me talk this evening and in the morning."

His room, Ann guessed as she washed in the large white pottery basin on the washstand, was probably the best in the hotel. And she was under no illusions as to why she had it. She was Ann Carruthers of the Vuelta Grant. Many of the Vuelta's financial and legal details had passed and would pass through the bank. But some other bank could be used. . . . Nevertheless, gratefully, she changed from the dove-gray traveling dress to a dinner dress of pale pink muslin, and hung tiny coral earrings in her ears. She was weary, stiff from the throw and jolt of the long, fast stage trip from Las Vegas. Yet she would not have missed this chance to freshen and change for an appearance in a town which seethed with boisterous life and strangers. The Vuelta Ranch was remote and isolated; any evening like this was welcome.

Tonight her light brown hair with glints of reddish gold did well enough piled loosely, almost carelessly, and pinned. In England she had ridden habitually. On the Vuelta, long days of riding had fined her slender figure almost to whip-wiriness. When she took Judge Bassett's arm outside her room, his admiration was sincere.

"Tonight, ma'am, I'll be the envy of Santa Fe."

"Lah!" Ann laughed, falling in with his mood. "It is I, sir, who will be envied for my escort!"

In the small lobby, strange men gave quick, approving stares. Best of all, keen feminine glances lingered on her with not exactly charitable interest.

The man who spoke to them had the same swift approval of Ann. "Miss Carruthers . . . Judge, sir . . . ?"

Ann said, smiling, "Mr. Roddan." This was Simon Roddan, from whom they had bought the Vuelta Grant.

"Simon. How are you?" the judge said.

"Envious," Simon Roddan admitted, smiling down at Ann.

He was a big man, reasonably young, a jocular, sometimes excessively friendly lawyer and politician, well on his way, Ann had heard, to being one of the most influential and wealthiest men in the Territory.

She had heard more, relayed mostly by Geoffrey. Simon Roddan had ridden in the Indiana cavalry under General Sherman in the march to Savannah and on north, when Sherman's coolly planned policy had drawn a wide swath of looted destruction through the unprotected vitals of the South. Gold, silver, jewels, small articles of high value had not been in Sherman's orders to confiscate. But a few cold-thinking, relentless men, able somehow to sniff out hidden valuables on once-prosperous plantations and in large town houses, had come out of the late war far more prosperous than when they had enlisted or been drafted.

Simon Roddan had been a young, shabby Indianapolis lawyer when he enlisted. Brevetted captain quickly, his bravery in battle had never been questioned. He had been too reckless, if anything. But immediately after the war, Roddan had come west with ample funds. He had made a point of meeting the right people, had been admitted to the Territorial Bar, had entered politics, and started his rocketing rise to prominence and full fortune. As a lawyer, he had specialized in old Spanish and Mexican laws and land titles. In one bitterly fought court suit, he had won legal title to the Vuelta Grant which, later, Geoffrey and Ann had bought from him.

Roddan's war years had been talked about by two drifters who had been in his command during the Georgia campaign. The enlisted men, the drifters had said, had called him "Bummer" Roddan after the foragers who had ranged far out on all flanks of Sherman's columns, scouring the countryside like a plague of ravenous grasshoppers. Such "bummers" had poured in each evening to Sherman's supply lines corn and hay, meal and flour, hams and bacon, beeves, horses, mules, the contents of root cellars, storerooms and often houses. "Bummer" Roddan, the two drifters had said, had been interested only in gold, silver, and precious stones, seldom food. Several times after talks inside large plantation houses, he had ordered the looted food put back, saying these people were northern sympathizers.

One of the hard-drinking, loud-talking drifters had been shot, the other one had vanished — but such yarns about a rising figure in the Territory had lingered under the surface, spreading. They did no real harm to Roddan. A man was judged by what he did now. But Simon Roddan reminded Ann of a tall, powerful, smiling buccaneer. Just looking at him made her pulse quicken although, vaguely, she disliked him because of the "bummer" stories — and Geoffrey's verdict. "A chap who'd swap a hungry, frightened, helpless lady's food back to her for her pearls would go for a baby's jugular any time he was hungry enough," Geoffrey had said calmly. "This is one man we need to watch — and continue watching."

Now Simon Roddan looked as if he could present pearls as he asked, smile widening, "Is your brother in

29

town, Miss Carruthers?"

"I came from the ranch alone."

"Then another evening, perhaps, I can hope for the pleasure, also? Tomorrow evening . . . ?"

"I'm not certain what tomorrow will bring, Mr. Roddan."

"I'll count on it." Roddan ducked his head, widening his smile further, making a promise out of a vague politeness.

Judge Bassett chuckled as they went on through the lobby to the busy dining room. "I suspect, young lady, you have a dinner engagement tomorrow night. Roddan is persistent and persuasive."

"He's been paid for the ranch, as you know," Ann reminded calmly. "There are no further obligations. And . . . persistence seldom persuades me."

"Simon is used to having his own way. He usually does."

"So am I . . . so do I," Ann said lightly.

Their table in the dining room was for two, tucked away in a corner. Ann asked the waitress for steer beef, roasted, a small baked potato, a fresh garden vegetable, and declined Bernalillo wine which Judge Bassett suggested. He ordered the inevitable steak, thick, rare.

When the waitress left, Ann handed him the note she'd brought — Geoffrey at his vaguest and gayest.

The whiskey is still less than top hole — as usual! The señoritas continue smiling — as usual. I am thinking of investigating an interesting proposal. Look for me when you see me — as usual. I will write. Your attentive brother — as usual,

Geoffrey

30

"Mailed in Mesilla many weeks ago — and nothing since," Ann said. "You will recall, sir, I wrote you some time ago asking if Geoffrey had communicated with you."

A line had etched between the judge's bushy brows. "No word has come from the young man. I suppose you know he carried a draft on our bank for five thousand dollars?"

"He didn't mention it." Frowning, Ann inquired, "Has he used the draft?"

"Not," said the judge, "that we've been advised. Your brother was also amply provided with cash funds, carried in a money belt."

"Why should he have traveled south with so much money?"

The judge's expression went mildly wry. "Your brother, Miss Carruthers, was a reserved young gentleman in many ways. He confided very little to me."

"Or anyone. It's a family trait."

"Did he like to gamble?"

"No! You . . . you said, 'did he?' As if you think. . . ."

"I'm merely puzzled."

"Judge Bassett . . . is it good or bad that Geoffrey seems not to have used that draft?"

"I don't know," the Judge admitted. "Using the draft would have given some indication of where he was and what, possibly, he was doing." He fell silent, then seemed to choose his words. "I wish you had advised me of all this much sooner."

"What could you have done?"

"Communicated with our contacts at Mesilla, Las Cruces, and both sides of the river at Paso del Norte."

"Letters!" Ann burst out. "Always Geoffrey has written me! His 'reserve' isn't deep enough to hold back any trouble which could have caused him to vanish this way.

31

Something has happened. I . . . I believe you're certain of it, also!"

Bassett ignored her outburst. "In two weeks or less, replies to inquiries should be in hand."

"Two weeks?" Ann was emphatic. "In two weeks I'll have inquired personally at Mesilla and other places in that part of the Territory and Texas!"

"My dear young lady. . . ."

"I've waited too long now!"

Judge Bassett was disturbed. He leaned forward earnestly. "I must advise against it. Even the stagecoach trip to Mesilla is dangerous. Apaches, Comanches, Kiowas are robbing, killing, burning in all that border country."

"Geoffrey," Ann reminded, "reached Mesilla in good health."

Bassett tapped the fingertips of one hand on the table for emphasis. His clean-shaved face made him look somewhat younger than he surely must be. "I don't want to increase your worry, Miss, but whatever your brother's health on reaching Mesilla, you have not heard from him since."

"Which is why I must go."

"Let me send a man who can search more thoroughly and safely than an unescorted young lady."

"That border country," Ann reminded, "must have a sheriff."

"It has. Mesilla is a county seat. Doña Ana County."

"And deputies, marshals, businessmen, military officers, and others who might help me."

"All those can be found," Bassett admitted with stubborn reluctance. "But travelers are still in great danger. The Las Cruces newspaper recently stated that nine out of ten cases in probate court were of deaths caused by Indians. Young lady . . . listen to an older man. Don't start a reckless search like this alone."

The waitress was coming with a loaded tray. "He's my brother. The stage for Mesilla leaves in the morning. I will need a bank draft, also, smaller than Geoffrey carried . . . and more cash money than I have with me."

"I've no choice," Bassett assented reluctantly. "I will ask for signed instructions from you so that the bank will know what to do in case you also drop out of sight."

"Of course."

"I remind you again," said Judge Bassett with dignity, "the Vuelta Grant is not a toy. Not the small homestead of an immigrant. Your brother and yourself have undertaken great responsibility, not to mention a small fortune in British exchange already expended on the ranch."

"I understand all that," Ann agreed soberly. "Just, please, don't suggest that I miss the stagecoach for La Mesilla tomorrow."

For a long moment the judge stared at her and, as the waitress reached them, he said under his breath, "You are stubborn, young lady!"

Ann's quick, flashing smile did not immediately wipe away his annoyed gravity.

Two more things happened that evening of which Ann was unaware. Simon Roddan sat in one of the bullhide chairs in the hotel lobby, cigar between his fingers, and pondered a note which had arrived in yesterday's mail.

No sign of him has showed yet.

That was all the note said. It was unsigned. Such odd, unusual, usually brief missives, came almost daily to his Santa Fe office. Usually some sort of a name, often false,

33

was signed to them.

Army life in the late war had taught Simon Roddan the value of information. Secret information. An army was only as deadly as its enemy. From his first months in the Territory, Roddan had cultivated sources of information. A favor done here, money judiciously lent there, trouble helped, leaving an obligation to be repaid, promises of rewards in one way or another. Much of the information that came in was harmless and useless at the time. Now and then an opportunity was opened. More importantly, more than one man's secret weaknesses, little treacheries and dishonesties, were relayed to Roddan — and filed away in memory until needed, if ever.

This man who had reported from the Vuelta Ranch had not been placed there by Roddan for any particular purpose. But the amounts of British exchange being invested in the ranch by two people who obviously knew little about such things deserved watching. When the occasional reports said that young Carruthers was off on a trip that drew into weeks, then months, Roddan had grown increasingly interested.

Tonight the girl had parried a casual question about her brother, giving the false suggestion that the brother was on the Vuelta Ranch. Why? Like a gently sniffing, mildly inquisitive hound of sharp nose, Roddan lounged in the bullhide chair, savoring his cigar and thoughtfully examining the matter from all sides.

When Judge Bassett left the hotel this same night, he cut across the noisy plaza, ignoring the rising hubbub of Santa Fe's night life with wagon trains in town. The alley into which he presently turned was filled with wan moonlight. Deep dust muffled footsteps. His rap on a solid plank door with light showing under the bottom edge was not answered. He knocked harder.

"Oh, Zeke! This is Bassett!"

"Whyn't you say so?" grumbled a voice inside, and the owner was still grumbling as the door opened. "Dern drunks come lookin' for gals half the night."

A short, bony little man, Zeke had an oversize, fierce white mustache, a ragged chin beard, red galluses, and the sleeves of a red undershirt pushed up on skinny, corded arms.

A cot stood against one wall of the small room. Dead wood ashes were gray in a corner fireplace. The floor was dry, pounded dirt. Two horizontal poles hung from the log ceiling vigas, Indian style, and held blankets, clothes and other articles. A small glass coal-oil lamp on a deal table shed light on a layout of solitaire cards.

"Zeke, why the devil don't you come over to the hotel and have dinner with me more often?"

"Too much washin' up an' gittin' ready. Told you so before."

"I need a favor from you, Zeke."

"A ol' has-been like me can't do much."

"Tomorrow, Zeke, a girl will be on the Mesilla stage — a young English girl. Her brother left on a trip, wrote her from Mesilla and then seems to have vanished. Against my advice, she insists on going to Mesilla and making a search for him."

"Sounds like you want her nurse-maided."

"Without her knowing it, Zeke. She'd not like it."

"Goin' soft-headed in your old age, ain't you? Humerin' gals! Beggin' favors from the likes of me."

"Strictly business, you old wolf. This girl and her brother bought the Vuelta Grant from Simon Roddan. They're valuable customers of the bank."

"I mind that deal. 'Bummer' Roddan thieved the Grant offen the real Mex owners, 'n' peddled it to these young pilgrims."

"With a legal and valid title. . . ."

"He still thieved it. You know so."

"I don't know any such thing. I can't sit in judgment on what the courts of this Territory do. Also, Roddan is a valued customer of the bank."

"Makes him a lily-white, huh? Money'n his pocket 'n' money in yours."

They had shared blankets together in the old days. Colin Bassett said, "Damn you, Zeke, will you go to Mesilla?"

"All that washin' up and dressin' up and nurse-maidin' a gal who don't want no nurse-maidin'?"

"Yes!"

Zeke's cackle shook his small bony frame. "It'll beat sittin' here alone with a greasy solitaire deck."

Chapter Three

It was another wine-like morning with scattered scraps of fleecy clouds hanging under a cobalt sky. The departing stagecoach rocked sedately on its leathers through the wagon-clogged south side of the Santa Fe plaza. Simon Roddan, standing on the planks in front of Meyer's Saddle Shop, talking to a client, ignored the outbound stage until an eye corner barely noted a feminine profile on the back seat.

His head jerked around, staring, making certain. A twinge of frustrated anticipation followed. No dinner with her tonight. She could have said she was going home. But — that wasn't the Barlow & Sanderson stage. That was a J.F. Bennet stage out of Las Cruces, rolling south now for days toward Paso del Norte.

Roddan knew that the girl's brother was missing from the Vuelta Ranch. Last night she had evaded admitting so. Now, in haste — for she had arrived only yesterday, late — she was traveling south!

Some five minutes later, in the Golondrina Bar west of the plaza, Roddan found the man he wanted. Only four customers were in the long, dim, cavernous room this early in the morning. The man lounging at the back curve of the bar finished his drink and came leisurely forward when he saw Roddan step in and jerk a head in summons.

Flat-faced and muscular, with high cheek planes, a gash of a mouth, a trimmed black mustache shot with gray, the man wore black broadcloth, a flowered silk vest crossed by a gold watch chain and carried two guns in shoulder holsters. His eyes were bloodshot; he needed a shave.

"A gully-buster night!" he said in a hoarsely flat voice. "After daylight before I got some sleep." He yawned. "I can use more."

"Not today," Roddan said curtly. "The Paso Norte stage just pulled out. I want you on it!"

"Bustin' out all over with wants, ain't you?" the flat, hoarse voice countered. "What's gone is gone — stage or booze."

"Throw a saddle on a horse! With luck, you can catch that stage at La Bajada station. If not, then at the next relay. Swap horses if you have to. I want a passenger on that stage followed. I want to know where she goes, what she does, who she talks to."

"She?"

"A lady, I'll add! Not a dance-hall floozy! Remember that, Cultus! A lady! She's not to suspect she's being followed. Her name is Miss Ann Carruthers. She and her brother bought the Vuelta Grant. The brother seems to have dropped out of sight. This sister may be going to meet him. I want a report every day or so, when possible."

"What about the brother?" Cultus asked indifferently.

Roddan stood very still for a moment, caught by a thought. "The brother?" His shrug followed. "He's in good health. I'd be willing to bet on that."

Alertness jumped into the bloodshot eyes, as if talk like this had been heard before. "You'd bet?" Cultus asked carefully.

"Why not?" Roddan said casually.

"How much you bet?"

Roddan licked his lips. "I'd bet a thousand dollars the brother's health is good and stays good."

"Some men get took right sudden," Cultus said coolly. "What about the girl? You want to bet on her health?"

Simon Roddan swallowed. "No, damn you, Cultus! Her health doesn't concern me. I merely want her watched."

For the space of three slow breaths the thin-lipped smile surveyed him. "We got a bet made," Cultus said. "An' I'll watch the girl close, seein' as she'll take me to her brother, looks like. Right now I need money to follow her."

"All you need," Roddan assented.

THE SOUTHERN OVERLAND MAIL & EXPRESS LINE of First Class Concord Coaches From Santa Fe to La Mesilla would hold memories later on of sweet safety and delicious comfort. Even the blistering ninety-mile trip through the waterless *Journado del Muerto* — The Journey of the Dead Man the cackling, amusing little old man on the seat across from Ann had called it — when throats parched, lips cracked, and the threat of raiding Apaches was real and present each hour was something she could look back upon later with nostalgia. But since she could not see into the future, the present was all that mattered. The blessed present when the dusty, creaking stagecoach finally wheeled into the bare plaza of Mesilla.

They drew up with a grinding of brake shoes on iron tires before the Traveler's House, which offered overnight accommodations to the many passengers who were traveling on from Mesilla into the far reaches of the border country.

Ann almost staggered when the smooth strong hand of her fellow passenger — a man named Jack Cultus, she had learned during the long trip — helped her off the coach step. She was the only woman passenger who had come all the way from Santa Fe, through days and nights of bouncing, jolting, swaying, dust-swirling heat and torment. Already she was beginning to understand some of Judge Bassett's apprehension. There was a barren, parched savageness about this southern border country which was lacking farther north. Here, even the earth, the distance, the lack of water and green growth, had a brassy glare which seemed implacable.

The short, bony little man with the ragged chin beard had hopped nimbly down before them, and was watching with a snag-toothed grin that showed a red cavern of mouth between ragged beard and mustache. His name was Zeke Winn. Day or night he seemed the same, a wrinkled, dark-parchment face with a pointy nose, small hands almost delicately formed despite the large blue veins and wrinkles of age, and an ill-fitting salt-and-pepper suit which hung on his skinny frame like a misshapen sack.

Old Zeke Winn never seemed to weary. He remained cheerful. Some of the barbed remarks he made to Jack Cultus showed that they knew one another and were not too friendly. Cultus had more or less sneered at and ignored the old man, who seemed unruffled by it.

Now old Zeke Winn's red cavern of a mouth grinned at her. "You come through with all your hair, Miss. Somethin' t' cel'brate."

"I'm going to celebrate by stretching out full length and taking a quiet nap," Ann said, smiling at the amusing little old man.

Cultus had turned away, obviously not further interested, and, when Ann went inside the adobe building, there was an immediate room for her. And a bed. She dropped on the straw-stuffed mattress with a grateful groan.

A dusty, crimson sun had been inching down to the western horizon when the stagecoach rolled into town. Ann could have slept on the lumpy straw mattress for hours. But after a short rest, her nagging fears about Geoffrey drove her to the wash basin, and into fresh, undusty clothes, and back into the cramped lobby of this small hotel.

The register was a dog-eared ledger. She had the date of Geoffrey's letter from Mesilla. Leafing back in the register three days before that date, she found his name in Geoffrey's blessedly familiar scrawl.

G. Carruthers, La Vuelta Ranch, Canimongo, N.M.T.

Her eyes misted. Here was Geoffrey; his writing, at least. The clerk, who was also the owner, had been lounging behind the short length of counter, stroking a bushy gray mustache, munching a thick cud in his cheek while he watched her silently.

"This man, Mr. Carruthers, is my brother," Ann said, tapping the line. "Can you tell me where I can find him?" And it did seem that, somehow, miraculously, Geoffrey must be close.

The clerk turned the dog-eared book around and studied the name, slowly chewing his tobacco. "Be the young Englishman, wouldn't he?"

"Yes."

"Stayed with us nigh a week."

"Where did he go? Did he say?"

The man shifted the bulging quid into the other cheek.

41

"Thinkin' back," he recalled slowly, "don't seem to me he said much about anything."

"Please," Ann said, and knew her voice was slightly husky now with strain and weariness, "please, can't you think back to something he said — to someone he knew here in Mesilla — who could give me an idea of where he is?"

"Sister, hah?" The man flipped the pages to her own signature.

Miss Ann Carruthers, La Vuelta, Canimongo, New Mexico Terr.

"Ain't that I doubted you, ma'am, but one time the lady was a man's wife, trackin' him. He wasn't kindly to me for talkin' when they come back through."

"Mr. Carruthers is not running from anything," Ann said coldly. "But I don't think he left here without hinting at his destination to someone."

"Seems reasonable, don't it?" came from behind her. Ann turned quickly. Old Zeke Winn, in the baggy salt-and-pepper suit, was silently laughing. He had come without sound, with the unabashed assurance of an old man.

"Mr. Todé there don't know nothin' or he'd have told you," old Zeke said amiably. "Chances are your young feller left sign. Even an Apache'll do it. Want a ol' has-been with time on his hands to throw in an' he'p you?"

"Oh, I wouldn't bother you."

Zeke Winn cackled. "Course not; you want he'p?"

"Yes, I do, Mr. Winn."

"Your brother gamble much?"

"No, indeed!"

"Booze?"

"He liked a drink at proper times."

"You mean he didn't get stinkin' . . . ?"

"I beg your pardon?"

"Drunk?"

"Certainly not!"

"He ever chase dance-hall gals?"

"I'm sure not. What kind of depraved. . . ."

"Ain't he'pin me gettin' all bridled about it," cut in Zeke Winn cheerfully. "A huntin' man has got to know what he's huntin'. Whyn't you stay comfortable here, Miss, whilst I mosey around town cuttin' sign?"

Ann hesitated, then good sense suggested that this amusing little old man just possibly might trace Geoffrey in this town quicker than she could.

"I will," Ann promised. She had an odd thought that one of the bright old eyes in the dark-parchment face winked slightly before he went out with a flat-footed shuffle of old age which, surprisingly, made almost no sound.

"He's very kind, even if he doesn't accomplish anything," Ann said, smiling now at Mr. Todé, the clerk.

He gave her a peculiar look. "Miss, don't you know him?"

"A Mr. Winn. He boarded the stage at Santa Fe."

"Zeke Winn," said the hotel man, and something like awe crept into his voice. "One of the last of the mountain men, ma'am. He was close to Jim Bridger and Carson. Fremont thought Zeke was as good as Carson and said so. He's been trapper and meat hunter, scout and lawman. He's done everything. Ain't a place in the West he ain't been."

"He . . . he talks like a poor old man about to take to his bed forever."

"This is the second time he's been here this year. The

43

other time the sheriff sent for him to track some horse thieves. They didn't seem to be Indians. Zeke trailed all the way up into Colorado. Had to kill one man. He got most of the horses back. Sold 'em in Colorado for the local owners and sent back the money. I've been wondering," said the clerk, "what thieves he's going to trail next."

Ann murmured, "I wouldn't have believed it." Somewhat chastened she returned to her room. She was relieved, also, and hopeful now. If anyone could locate Geoffrey, this Zeke Winn surely must be the man.

Chapter Four

These were the nights when the moon was waxing full. Nights of the great silver Comanche Moon. Far over in Texas where settlers had pushed their cabins and soddies out into the grassy billows of the plains, smoke lifted high into the midday glare. A woman, clutching a baby, fled in a frenzy of fear out the rear of a cabin, past the shabby little corral, grass whipping at her long skirts. Two painted horsemen followed her and rode her down.

Two days distant that same night, obscene tongues of crimson fire licked toward the coldly placid moon. The remote miles swallowed the increasing obscenity of shots, whoops, agonized screams.

In hundreds of other cabins over immense reaches of frontier, other men and women watched tensely through the long nights, finding no beauty in the great glowing orb that drenched the land with frosty light. These were the nights, the days when the Comanches and Kiowas rode far and fast, raiding, killing.

South of the Rio Bravo — which some men called the Rio Grande — far south into Chihuahua, the same silver disk dusted light on the rugged mountains and grassland, and fields, gardens, walls of a large hacienda. But at this hacienda there was a difference. Tense and fearful waiting were lacking inside the pink and blue and white-tinted walls. Full moon or dark-of-the-moon made little dif-

45

ference, save in the beauty of the nights.

The reasons were the high, guarded wall topped with shards of broken glass, the massive gate closed, barred from darkness to sunrise. And, finally, the Yellow Hairs. Enemies without or within the hacienda were dealt with savagely and efficiently by the Yellow Hairs. And anyone who crossed the will of Don Alfredo Correon de Leon y Delgado was an enemy.

South of the Bravo, but not far south, where the small run of water murmured past cottonwoods and salt cedars, the two cook fires became three fires, then five . . . eight. And still more war parties rode in, summoned by fast riders and smoke signals. Fifty . . . sixty . . . even a hundred miles a day could be covered by these raiding Quahada Comanches who were gathering south of the Bravo under Juan Tomás.

There was talk and planning. Juan Tomás harshly refused to let the hot-headed younger men start riding deeper into Chihuahua.

"We wait!"

He had led them before to loot and captives. They waited. The older men gathered with Juan Tomás and talked, carefully plotting this great raid deep into Chihuahua where the Yellow Hairs had killed or captured Juanito, the son of Juan Tomás.

Ann had eaten and was resting again in her hotel room. One did not in several hours repair the battering of hundreds of miles of rough coach travel. Outside the single room window the night was flooded with white moonlight. Ann could see without lighting the coal-oil lamp.

Her mind would not rest. Now that she was in Mesilla, the mystery of Geoffrey's trip here was only compounded.

46

What could have brought him so far from the Vuelta Ranch and Santa Fe? With a bank draft? With a stuffed money belt? What interesting proposal had he come to investigate? Only to vanish!

A rap on the door brought Ann off the bed, instinctively patting her hair. Moonlight poured through the window. She opened the door without lighting the lamp. A hall lamp in a wall bracket was burning wanly. And Old Zeke Winn standing there said, "I figgered you'd want some word afore morning."

"Have you discovered anything?"

"Might be."

"Please come in. I'll light the lamp."

Even now, as added light bloomed through the room, it was not easy to cast this man as the near-legendary figure the clerk had described.

The parchment-wrinkled face, the inoffensive droop of shoulders inside the shabby salt-and-pepper suit helped the appearance of meekness as he stepped inside and inquired, "Ever hear of a man named Roybal?"

"No."

"Never heard your brother speak of him?"

"I'm sure not."

"I found a bartender remembered your brother talkin' to a man. The barkeep heard your brother say, 'I intend to follow the suggestion you made in Santa Fe, Mr. Roybal. I'm going to Paso del Norte, and on to Azul.' "

"Azul?" Ann repeated.

"You ever heard him speak of Azul?"

"Never!"

"It's a relay station for the Chihuahua stages. An' a place where you cut off to the big Delgado hacienda."

"Is . . . is this man Roybal in Mesilla now?" None of it made sense.

47

Zeke Winn's shoulders moved in a silent chuckle. But his eyes had clear, cool inquiry.

"You never let on that you knowed Jack Cultus."

"The gentleman who caught the stage at La Bajada, this side of Santa Fe?"

"Yep."

"I had never seen the man before he climbed into the stage at La Bajada. Or heard of him."

"Cultus had already asked the barkeep an' others about your brother. Cultus an' me was cuttin' sign on the same man tonight."

"But . . . I don't understand. I did not mention Geoffrey on the stagecoach. Or at any other time to this man Cultus. Why should he be trying to help me?"

"Jack Cultus never heped anybody but Jack Cultus," said Zeke Winn dryly.

"Who is he?"

"Mean an' tough. You got no idea why he might be askin' about your brother?"

"I can't even guess," Ann said slowly. The knot of worry inside was balling tighter now.

"Cultus has hauled out," Zeke Winn said. "Give up his room, hired a fast team an' buggy at the livery, an' left town. That's what took me so long, runnin' sign on him, too."

"I don't understand, Mr. Winn."

"Makes two of us, then," Zeke Winn admitted amiably. "But if Jack Cultus ain't headin' for Azul, I never guessed worse."

"The important thing is that Geoffrey planned to go to this place — this Azul — and evidently did, and has not returned."

"He might have, then gone some'eres else."

"The stage station in Paso del Norte or at Azul could

tell me. Thank you, Mr. Winn, so much."

He lingered. "Sounds, ma'am, like you mean to go clean to Azul."

"I do, if necessary."

"It ain't a good idea. Old Mexico ain't New Mexico."

"If differences in people and customs were so important, I would have remained in England."

"Ma'am, I ain't talkin' about eatin' chili or drinkin' tequila or mescal. Take this Delgado hacienda. You ever hear about a big Mejicano hacienda run the old way?"

"I have been on estates in Spain."

"I ain't," said Zeke Winn. "But I can tell you about a big hacienda like that'n you reach from Azul. Anywhere in that Azul country, what the Delgados say is law. A Delgado man can borry a man's wife or daughter an' the poor devil is honored! They can whip a man, hang a man, shoot a man! They even got their own soldiers. Good ones, too. The law is what they say it is. That just ain't a place for a strange young lady to poke around with questions."

"Are you trying to say, Mr. Winn, that something could have happened to Geoffrey and it might be dangerous for his sister to cross the border and inquire?"

"I thought I spoke plain."

"Mexico," Ann reminded with slight asperity, "is a civilized country. In England, I have met people from Mexico. They were educated, charming and gracious. One wouldn't wish to know nicer people."

"Ma'am," said Zeke Winn humbly, "I'm just a ol' has-been, not fittin' for much." He had killed one man already this year. He had trailed outlaws clear up into Colorado. "I got business takin' me to Paso del Norte and Azul," Zeke Winn said meekly. "If you wouldn't mind me taggin' along when you go, it might be you could sort of look out for me."

Ann frowned. Then her laughter came. "You fraud! You admirable, lovable fraud! I would feel so much better if you were near me, Mr. Winn."

Chapter Five

It was early in the evening when the same two Yellow Hair hacienda guards brought Geoffrey Carruthers back to the adobe prisoners' hut. The two huge water wheels outside the hut were motionless, quiet for the night. The half-wild watch dogs were tied outside. Their savage barking rose to a crescendo as horses approached, and quieted reluctantly when Big Luis cursed them and struck a time or two with his whip.

O'Meara, the burly Irishman, next to Hardisty inside the hut, said softly, "I wonder if it was his sister come on the hacienda? Sure now, even the thought of it like to broke him down."

"Can't blame him," Hardisty said briefly.

"Still wearin' his jewelry," O'Meara decided a moment later.

They could hear the metallic clink-jingle of Carruthers's wrist and leg chains still riveted on. But the flooding moonlight in the gaping doorway, and light from a lantern, brought an added grunt from O'Meara.

"Faith! The man's a dude now! Lookit him!"

Hardisty was already staring from where he sat on the hard-packed dirt floor. Geoffrey Carruthers had bathed and shaved. His long, matted hair had been cut. The ragged pants and filthy, ripped shirt had been replaced by a peon's new white manta cloth pants and loose shirt.

Now the Englishman's gaunt, ravaged face could be clearly judged. The guards were passing the long prisoners chain between Carruthers's shackled legs and securing the end of the chain to the thick, upright post outside the doorway. One guard mocked in Spanish, using Don before the last name in insult.

"The *Señor Don Carrrrutherrrrs* will want more tonight?"

Carruthers ignored him.

"*Con Dios y el diablo,*" the guard said, catching up the lantern and starting out. "With God and the devil — until *mañana* when the *patrón* sees you again."

O'Meara's envious brogue cut through the moonlight which reached through door and window openings.

"Aguardiente! Smell it on the man! Perfume of the devil! And more of it, maybe, tomorrow, when they take him out again. Arrrgh! Poteen! Like one of the family!"

"Let him alone. He's one of the family here," Hardisty reminded.

The long chain that secured them all was spiked to a log buried deep at the far end of the room. From that log the chain ran the length of the room, and out the door to the upright section of log around which it made several turns before it was locked. A lighted lantern hung there, a guard was on duty all night, and the dogs were always close.

Carruthers, the last one on the chain, was nearest the door tonight. Hardisty was at his right. Then O'Meara. Then Juanito, the Quahada Comanche prisoner. The other prisoners, dull and hopeless hacienda peons, were farther along on the chain.

"Was the lady visitor really your sister?" Hardisty asked quietly.

"She was."

"You talked with her?"

"No!"

Now they were all sitting on the pounded dirt floor, where they would sleep, also. Hardisty's wrist chains chinked softly as he rolled a shuck cigarette which prisoners were allowed. Carruthers did the same. O'Meara followed suit.

The first flaring match showed again the gaunt strain and sadness on Carruther's face. "Ann," he said in a low voice, "doesn't know I'm on the hacienda. She merely thinks I may have come this way. She and some old man who's with her, guiding her."

"I guess," Hardisty confessed slowly, "I don't understand. You didn't talk to your sister, but you know what's in her mind?"

"You'll understand when I explain," Carruthers said bitterly. "First I was given a chance to clean up and shave, my hair was hacked shorter, and I was given these clothes and a decent meal."

"And Aguardiente," O'Meara said and smacked his lips.

"Yes," agreed Carruthers. "Aguardiente. Half a bottle if I wanted to drink it all."

O'Meara groaned with envy.

"I didn't," Carruthers said. "A towel was tied over my mouth. A guard took each arm. Another guard put a rope loop around my neck, in case I struggled. And then I was taken into a back entrance of the house and allowed to look past a balcony screen at Ann, who was dining like a guest of honor. She was seated at Delgado's right. She laughed at something he said. Then I was taken outside again, to a bench in the flower garden."

Hardisty said dryly, "I know that bench. Don Alfredo Delgado sat on it, smelling a flower in his hand, while

53

he questioned me, and had me beaten to get the answers he thought he'd get."

"He sat on the bench with me, most courteously, while a man was behind me holding the rope loop around my neck," said Carruthers dispiritedly. "We talked in English. Delgado seemed to think he was a reasonable man. It was, he explained once more, a family matter. Of honor as well as money. For generations — well over a hundred years — the Delgados had owned the Vuelta Grant, in New Mexico. Then gringo laws, dishonest lawyers, juries and judges — who most certainly had been bribed — had stolen the Vuelta from its rightful owners. And when Ann and I bought the grant, we became no less guilty, for we had bought stolen property, and must have known it. Which is how Delgado reasons."

"That's what would have happened in Chihuahua," Hardisty said.

"He said all that when I first came here," Carruthers said heavily. "He let me know I'd been tolled across the border with that man's yarn about cheap cattle and horses to stock the Vuelta Ranch. And all I had to do to return safely was to sell him half the Vuelta for a pittance."

O'Meara broke in, "An' if you lived to cross the border with a peso of it, a leprechaun would be El Presidente in Washington!"

"Exactly," Carruthers agreed. "But if Delgado had me killed between here and the border — and I'm certain he would — I can't see how he would make a suspicious tale like that hold up when Ann's lawyers took it to court. And they would. I know Ann."

In the distance, the eerie mournful howl of a coyote broke off into clamoring barks at the moon. Miles away a second coyote replied. Barks and snarls joined in from the uneasy watch dogs outside. The voice of Big Luis

54

cursed them quiet.

Juanito, the Comanche prisoner, finished rolling a shuck cigarette and struck a match flaring on an iron wrist cuff. He had been on his back, seemingly asleep. Now he was sitting up on the packed dirt with almost rigid interest. His eyes seemed to glow in the match light.

Hardisty drew deep on his own smoke and answered Carruthers.

"You have to remember one thing. Never forget it. Don Alfredo Delgado thinks Mexican. He can talk English, but he thinks like a hacienda don. Always what he has wanted here in Mexico has happened. So why shouldn't it happen north of the border? And he could be half right. With a sale paper like that, witnessed legally here in Mexico, he could cloud title to your Vuelta Ranch. He might sell the paper to someone else. Under the circumstances it would be foolish to put more money into your ranch. And Delgado would have only your sister for a partner. A mere woman could be bent to his wishes. Also he'd have the satisfaction of honor satisfied and partial recovery — to start with — of what he feels was stolen from him. All of it makes sense when you look at it through his eyes."

"Look at us!" O'Meara grated. "His prisoners! Worse than dogs in his eyes! Why shouldn't he think big? He rules the roost!"

Coyote clamor lifted again, closer. Once more Big Luis had to quiet the dogs outside. In the moonlight streaming through door and window openings, Hardisty watched the young Indian cant his head, listening intently to the distant coyotes.

Premonition and sudden excitement stirred in Hardisty. His pulses began to move faster. Were those real coyotes clamoring at the full moon? What was making the young

55

Quahada Comanche so intent? He had heard coyotes all his life.

Carruthers was saying bitterly: "Delgado couldn't break me on one of these wheels. Not enough to make me sign his damned papers. I think he was realizing it. But now, Ann is here on his hacienda. The man holds all the cards. All!"

"Did he make threats about her?"

"He didn't have to. The facts were behind his greasy politeness. Ann was here, now, also. Both she and I were helpless. He and I both understood that. Look what Delgado has done to me — and to you men — and other men! D'you doubt what he'll do now? To Ann?"

"The Delgado men have always had their way," Hardisty murmured. "It gets to be a habit."

Coyote clamor lifted again, still closer, setting off the dogs once more. The young Comanche's cigarette glowed brightly as he pulled on it almost viciously.

"Juanito?"

A grunt answered Hardisty.

He continued in English, since none of the peons farther along on the chain understood it. "Tonight the coyotes are many."

"Si."

"Two-legged coyotes," said Hardisty quietly. He made it a statement, not a question.

Juanito did not reply.

Hardisty had been speaking softly past O'Meara's shoulder. The Irishman also had gone rigid, but O'Meara held silence while his stare questioned Hardisty.

An owl hooted and a second owl hooted back. Juanito's cigarette glowed as he drew deeply.

Hardisty said gently, "Quahada or Apache, Juanito?"

"How I know?"

Now Hardisty was certain. Indians were on the hacienda. Out there in the bright moonlight. The hacienda guards, the Yellow Hairs, evidently did not know. There had been no shots. But — how many Indians? What did they mean to do? Run off a few horses?

The growing sense of tight excitement which was filling Hardisty brushed aside any theft of a few horses or mules. He was remembering that Juanito was son of Juan Tomás, great war chief of the Quahada Comanches. The chief whose mother had been white, whose favorite wife reputedly was white, thereby making Juanito more white than Indian. Juan Tomás, who could think and plan as coldly and carefully as any white man, would hardly come for a few horses when he had lost a son.

Still using English, Hardisty put a question. "If the Quahada come, will these prisoners die?"

"Do I know?" Juanito said.

Another owl hooted. Juanito pushed his cigarette end into the dirt floor and rolled another. This time the match flare showed a cat-glow in his eyes. Carruthers, weighted with fear for his sister, seemed unaware of what was happening. O'Meara understood.

"Laddie," O'Meara said to Hardisty, "tonight we get our throats cut, or we cut some throats! ¿Que no?"

"If we can get off this chain alive, and get this jewelry off our wrists and ankles."

"Don Alfredo keeps the shackle keys in the big house to make sure that no prisoner escapes. He told me so in one of our question periods, while he was assuring me I didn't have a chance to escape."

"And his men were using whips on you."

"I told them," Hardisty said, "to stop tickling me."

"The sons of filth!"

"A man is what he is. How is your chain link?"

57

"Here! Twist! I'll twist the other way!"

A cold chisel would quickly have parted any link. Only the fact that the link was grooved by months of patient work gave any chance for success. O'Meara strained one way; Hardisty wrenched the other way.

"It's bending!" Hardisty whispered.

Moments later the side of the link snapped free and the chain parted. Now Hardisty had both hands free. Most of the chain was hanging from one wrist. He took the spike and pushed the end into the abraded link in O'Meara's chain. It took longer, but finally the Irishman's link snapped open.

"Thanks be to God!" O'Meara blurted under his breath as both hands also swung free. "Now! Your ankle chain!"

They were gaining proficiency or the link on Hardisty's ankle chain was much weakened. It opened quickly. Hardisty had a rawhide string in his pocket, hoarded for this moment. As with his wrist, most of the ankle chain was attached to the right shackle. He wound the chain around the right ankle and lashed it there with the rawhide. When he stood up, he was a free man with a length of chain dangling from his right wrist. That, too, had been planned.

The coyotes had aroused the dogs once more. Big Luis, enraged, had come out into the open from the guards' shack and whipped the dogs into whimpering quiet. Now he bawled at the hut doorway, "Is it you sons of *putas* who keep these dogs awake? I think maybe a little whip inside there will give a man his sleep!"

"I'll handle him," Hardisty said from the corner of his mouth. He was still on his feet. Two steps took him over beside the doorway.

Big Luis snatched the lighted lantern outside and stepped into the hut, whip in hand. "Dogs will howl outside and inside!" Big Luis promised. His whip slashed viciously at the nearest figure, which was Carruthers.

The Englishman tried to grab the whiplash and missed.

"*¡Olé!* The *cabrón* fights! I will cut your skin off in little strips with the whip!"

"While the devil laughs!" Hardisty said in Spanish. He stepped forward, a shadowy, looming figure in the moonlight.

The chain dangled from Hardisty's right wrist shackle. It was gripped in his fist also now, for greater control. Cursing, Big Luis had wheeled to face this sudden threat of a voice and looming shadow.

The chain made a snake-like whisssssssh as it flashed up, then whipped down with a terrible slash squarely across the contorted face. Bleating in shock and pain as he staggered, Big Luis dropped the lantern and lifted his arm to shield himself from another blow. The chain was already whisssshing — back, up, and down — lashing over the up-flung arm, rusty links cutting, tearing skull and face of the big, sadistic guard.

Hardisty was using iron arm muscles and full weight behind the blows for he had to stop this man fast and completely. He chain-beat Big Luis down to hands and knees, and the man tried to scuttle to some safety with head hanging low, with animal-like mewlings, slobbering through blood spurting from his torn mouth.

O'Meara was still attached to the long prisoners' chain. He had enough freedom of movement to lunge over and grab the scuttling guard. O'Meara's fist clamped into the man's long, greasy hair. A yank brought Big Luis off balance and his head up. O'Meara's powerful hands shot in and settled around the neck.

"Got you finally!" the Irishman panted in a half-snarl.

59

Big Luis threshed and kicked on the dirt floor, clawing at O'Meara's hands, wildly, frenziedly throwing his weight around as he tried to break away.

"Knew if I waited long enough. . . ." O'Meara gasped from the effort he was putting forth.

The cries and frantic screams that tore from the guard's chest were muted by O'Meara's hands around his neck. The strength began to run out of him. The sounds grew less and less, and slowly he quieted and went limp on the hard-packed dirt.

Still O'Meara held the neck to make sure. When he finally pushed it away with something like revulsion, he was panting and sweating.

"A long wait for that! Ahhhhh! The feel of it in me hands . . . like I've dreamed of when his whip was on our backs!" O'Meara turned back, picked up the spike again, and worked at the link on his leg chain.

"Good!" Juanito said. "Good! Good!" Hardisty knew that the myth of the unsmiling Indian was just that — a myth. If anything, Indians laughed more than white people. And in this moment Juanito let his feelings show fully. "He is first one," Juanito said in better English than he had admitted knowing. "There be more tonight — many more."

The dropped lantern had guttered out. Hardisty bent over, searched the guard's pockets, and found the key he wanted. He stepped through the doorway. A moment later he had the lock open and the prisoners' chain off the upright section of log. Now every prisoner inside was free to hobble off as his leg chain would permit. The peons were huddled fearfully at the end of the hut, not sure what was happening.

Carruthers, on his feet, said unsteadily, "That was fast. I must say, really corking."

Juanito moved into the doorway, ankle chain clinking. Standing in the full moonlight he lifted his head and hooted like an owl. From the bluff edge near the water wheels, another owl answered.

Carruthers was uncertain. "Are Indians really near?"

"Comanches, I'd guess, looking for Juanito."

"Will they attack us? Scalp us?"

"Possibly," Hardisty had to admit. "They don't like Mexicans or Americans."

"Or British, eh?"

"I guess they never heard of Britain. You'd better know. We can't do much to protect ourselves. Delgado wouldn't allow guns here at the water wheels, in case prisoners broke free somehow and got the guns. Useless to try escape. By the sounds, coyotes and owls, Indians all around us. Could mean a knife or a bullet any step."

"Frying pan into the fire." Geoffrey Carruthers's slight attempt at humor faded. "The big house," he remembered. "Ann, my sister, is there. Aren't all of them in danger? The stories I've heard about Indian attacks and . . . and helpless women. . . ."

What could a man say to such thoughts? The stories about Indian attacks were true. Horror stories about women, children, babies, grown men!

"The main house has that thick, high wall topped with broken glass," Hardisty reminded. "The front gates are guarded day and night. Apaches, Comanches, and other tribes have raided this hacienda more than once. None seem to have even got at the big house. It's a fort."

Carruthers said with relief, "Makes me feel slightly better."

What good to tell the man his sister would be as safe with the Comanches as with Don Alfredo de Leon y Delgado? Both the Comanches and Delgado lacked mercy

61

when it suited their purpose.

The owls were talking again. Juanito, outside the doorway, was answering. Riders came with a muffled rush into the bluff-girdled cul-de-sac where the water wheels were located. The fierce dogs were killed with lance thrusts. The night outside the huts filled with the click-grunt-gobble of Comanche talk.

Juanito was answering when a new man rode up. In the moonlight, he was a barrel-chested warrior wearing a skin shirt, who swung down and gave Juanito a big hug. That, Hardisty made a quick guess, would be the famous war chief, Juan Tomás. Hardisty was standing in the doorway now, watching. Flanking him were O'Meara and Carruthers, watching in silent intentness, also.

Juanito held up his chained wrists in the moonlight, then indicated his chained ankles and jerked his head back at the doorway as he talked rapidly in Comanche.

The barrel-chested warrior spoke in deep terseness. "Come out, white men."

"Here we go," said Hardisty under his breath. "Let me do the talking. One man will do better than three." As he stepped out, Hardisty said calmly, "You're Juanito's father, Chief Juan Tomás — no? And you talk and understand English about as well as I do, I've heard."

The chest on the man was sheer brute power. More than the son had, who was wiry and on the slender side. Aquiline features and high cheekbones, the same as Juanito had, were white blood. Bold nose hooked over a wide, stern-looking mouth. Gunbelt and repeating rifle were ready for quick use. His stare through the moonlight at Hardisty showed neither like nor dislike.

"Juan Tomás talk little English," he conceded. "Name you have?"

"Hardisty."

Juan Tomás pointed with his chin. "You?"

"O'Meara."

"You?"

"Carruthers."

Juanito spoke in Comanche. His father said, "Hardisty. How you break that chains?"

"O'Meara and I have been working on them for months. Carruthers here, and Juanito, have not. There are," Hardisty said coolly, "only two other ways to get them off. A hammer, chisel and files from the blacksmith shop back of the big house — or the keys to these iron cuffs from Don Alfredo Delgado."

"Juanito no ride horse like this."

"He won't ride far with ankles chained together like that," Hardisty agreed.

Juan Tomás spoke without anger or boasting, in astonishingly good English.

"We get keys from this Mex'can, then put 'em fire-hot down his throat. He is in house. We have two his men tell us so."

"Two Yellow Hairs? The guards with yellow calfskin vests, the hair outside?"

"Two men with . . . with cow wagons."

"Cow . . . you mean ox carts?"

"Si. I forget that name, 'ox.' "

"You're going to try to get past the high wall, into the big house?"

Juan Tomás sounded calmly confident.

"We burn. Kill. Take women an' ever't'ing. I promise so my people."

"How many men have you got?"

"Many."

Hardisty was blunt.

"Take my advice. Don't try too much. Those hacienda

guards that they call Yellow Hairs are many, too. Many guns. Good fighters. They've fought Indians before. They obey orders. They have all the hacienda buildings to fort up in and fight. If fires are started, they'll have light to see Comanches. Kill Comanches."

"All that," said Juan Tomás, "is in my mind."

"Think of this, then. This hacienda was here before your grandfather's fathers. Many Indians have come to kill and burn. Where are they now? What did they kill? What did they burn? The hacienda is still here. The big house is over there behind its high wall."

"I have t'ink of that."

"Can you break down the heavy front gates fast? Quickly? If you don't know where the Yellow Hairs are — all of them — you may be whipped before you get past those front gates."

The smile Juan Tomás gave him had a thin edge.

"One dam'-fool Indian, you t'ink, Hard'sty? No?"

"Juan Tomás is not the name of a damn-fool Indian. But Don Alfredo Delgado and his Yellow Hairs can make a fool out of any man who isn't sure what he's doing — and has a lot of luck. Big luck."

This time he was sure of the rusty chuckle.

"We have ladders. We bring pieces new cowhide for top wall. These *ranchero casas* are rabbit traps. Rabbits wait inside. We take. We kill."

"These rabbits have big teeth."

The rusty chuckle came again. Hardisty stared at the man, and slowly admitted, "You might do it . . . you might just do it." A new thought made him say with calculated coolness, "My wife — my woman — is a prisoner in that big house. I want to go in and get her." He held up his wrists. The chain was parted, but the shackles were still around his wrists. "I want to get the

64

keys from Don Alfredo Delgado."

"You have woman?" Juan Tomás grunted. "I t'ink you fight good then for woman. Juanito call you frien'. I, Juan Tomás, say, 'I you frien', like Juanito.' We take this Mex'can an' burn his rabbit nest. No?"

"O'Meara, too? And Carruthers?"

"*Sí.*"

The Comanche turned away, speaking to four men who had moved up behind him. Carruthers spoke worriedly at Hardisty's shoulder.

"Can't you tell him about my sister?"

"Don't speak of a sister," Hardisty said sharply under his breath. "She's my wife, now. My woman."

"Wife? Really, now. . . ."

"These Comanches may let me have a wife, a woman who is a prisoner here, also. They might let me have her if I can get in first and get her away. But if they get in that house first, any woman not killed will be up for grabs by any man who gets her and wants her. Will you understand that? Will you keep quiet and let me do what I can? Agree with everything I say and do?"

"Oh, yes! Of course. I . . . I didn't realize. . . ."

"The young lady," said O'Meara with wry humor, "will be surprised at how quick an' easy she got married."

Hardisty didn't bother to say what O'Meara must guess also: there was small chance of ever setting eyes on the girl. And this attempt to take the house with its high wall and gun guards would probably end in failure. But then, he wasn't Chief Juan Tomás. He wasn't giving orders tonight.

Chapter Six

The ladders the Comanches had made looked like travois poles with foot rungs only a few inches wide lashed on with fresh green cowhide. The wet, unsalted hide strands already were shrinking in the dry air and smelling.

Four ladders and two folded squares of raw cowhide had been brought to the hacienda, showing unusual patience and planning for horse Indians on a raid. Plainly the shrewd mind of Juan Tomás had conceived this extraordinary strategy of bringing ladders and the plan of how to use them.

When final moves had been decided, two ladders and a square of cowhide had been given to Hardisty and O'Meara. They would try to scale the wall well back toward the rear. Alone, they would try to enter the house, find the *patrón*, Don Alfredo de Leon y Delgado, and from him get keys to wrist irons and leg irons. All that, if possible, before the uproar of alarm started.

It was a hare-brained scheme, without much chance of success, Hardisty was forced to believe. And the same for his suggestion that he get Ann Carruthers and bring her out to her brother, and get her safely away from the hacienda in some, as yet unplanned, manner. But at least he and O'Meara had a chance to try. Juan Tomás wanted Juanito free to fight and ride astride a horse. Any man who rode north hundreds of miles through Mexico and Texas, through desert and mountains and plains, would need hands and feet unfettered.

It was that urgent need, Hardisty guessed, which made Juan Tomás amenable to advice, and willing to wait and risk this attempt to enter the big house. The Carruthers girl was a matter of indifference to Juan Tomás. The keys were wanted. Nothing else. So important did Juan Tomás consider the keys that he had provided Hardisty and O'Meara with shell belts and revolvers and holsters.

A waste of time to speculate about the belts and guns. The leather and the guns themselves had the much-used look and feel of work-a-day articles. Somewhere on the long, long frontier, lonely, crawling wagons had been ambushed. A cattle herd had been raided. An isolated cabin had vanished in crackling flames and swirling sparks and smoke. And the aftermath would have been like a garden fertilized with death. Would there, Hardisty wondered, ever be an end to it?

Near the big house, screened by the sheltering green vines of the extensive hacienda vineyard, O'Meara muttered his opinion.

"If we get the damn keys — and there ain't much chance of it — faith, we'll be in the damn Comanch' tribe! Be one of them. That Juanito, on the water wheels with us, puts an acey-duecey with him an' his old man. An' his old man is the big hairy rooster on this Indian roost, if I ever seen one."

"We're lucky," Hardisty agreed.

"But if we don't get the damn keys, our hair won't be so safe, even if we get back over the wall alive. . . ."

Hardisty lifted a ladder upright in the moonlight between the grape vines and tested it by stepping hard on the bottom rungs. They held.

"We'll need more than our luck if we get back over

the wall alive," he said quietly. "I tried to tell Juan Tomás. He's up against disciplined fighters in the Yellow Hairs. They've met Indians before. I doubt if they'll panic. They'll know what to do. That house and some of the other buildings are forts. Built for that. When the first shots are fired, these Indians will need strict discipline, too. I don't think they'll have it. They're brave. They'll fight and die. But. . . ."

"What about that girl? Carruthers's sister?"

"If the Comanches get inside the house, and she's not with me, she won't have a chance. We'll do what we can do. No more."

The moon was a great silver ball in a velvet sky — the night an immensity of empty distance flooded with moonlight. And in the emptiness there was life. Furtive life. Among the close-spaced vines in the large vineyard, unshod hoofs of buffalo ponies stamped restlessly on the quiet earth. Waiting ponies blew softly. Indians were gliding shadows.

O'Meara complained in disgust. "That square of green cowhide stinks like the devil's rotted hoof. And I got to carry it under my nose."

"Leave it here and get cut to pieces on that broken glass on top of the wall."

"Bleed or stink! I'll stink!"

In the distance another coyote broke into yapping clamor at the moon. Dogs in the clutter of huts, brush ramadas, outbuildings, and corral pens back of the big house barked furiously back at the wild sounds.

A shadowy figure came out of the vines. Juan Tomás said, "You go. Evert'ing wait 'til guns shoot. Inside, outside, guns shoot, we fight."

"You'd better fight good," said Hardisty evenly. He had no feelings at the moment for anything or anyone.

68

This was the chance to live, to escape from this vast hacienda and the complete ruthlessness of the Delgados. And even the small chance of escape might vanish if these Comanches lost control. It was as simple as that. Survival meant a successful raid, with the barbaric consequences to the hacienda. If the raid failed, the equally woeful medieval-barbarism of Don Alfredo Delgado, whose will was law, would take over.

Fatalism dropped on Hardisty as he and O'Meara advanced toward the big house. This night the iron will of Delgado would be crossed. Violently. Equally ruthlessly. They might die. Even O'Meara's volatile temperament understood the risks.

The burly Irishman was the older man, but Hardisty was giving orders. Beyond the vineyard, to the east, tall trees lined the hacienda road, which ran south here to the solid, thick wooden gates in the high wall around the big house. Well out from the house, forking off to the left, a rutted, dusty, much-used road skirted the house wall back to the headquarters area of the hacienda.

Back there were the dirt-floored huts and mud-plastered brush ramadas of the workers. The sheds and corrals, shops, storehouses, outbuildings. Back there were the fort-like barracks of the Yellow Hairs. And on beyond, right and left, were gardens and orchards, wine press and winery. Back there were men and women, children, babies, dogs. Horses and mules. Oxen and chickens. A small world of its own. And every chicken and fighting cock, every horse and dog, child and man and woman, belonged body and spirit to the Hacienda of Our Lady of Sorrows. To Don Alfredo Delgado. That knowledge helped harden a heart.

Every man or woman — probably every child past half-growth — would betray any outsider to the cold mercies

69

of the *patrón* of the hacienda, Don Alfredo. Or kill, if that were the *patrón*'s wish. The dogs would pull a stranger down and tear at him. The women, the children would scream alarm. The men would kill. All were an extension of the Delgado will. Mercy that any man might feel was blunted when his own life balanced against such odds.

At night, and during the day, also, two Yellow Hairs guarded the massive front gates. There was a gate house at one side. Fighting towers were built into each corner of the high walls. Rifle openings pierced the walls. The big house itself was a second fort, with iron grills at doors and windows. And back of the outer wall, beyond a smaller, barred rear gate, were the house stables and barns and the horse pens and fort-like barracks of the Yellow Hairs. It was a formidable defense when manned and ready.

But tonight it was not manned or ready. Or any night. Arrogant carelessness had developed through years of safety. The corner towers of the house wall were empty. The back gate was unwatched. The two guards at the front gate ignored the rest of the wall, and usually alternated in sleep.

All that, Hardisty had made it his business to know. A corner of the immense vineyard reached within two hundred yards of the house wall on this side. Moonlight flooded the open space. But the corner watch towers were not manned, the wall not patrolled.

The night coolness had settled in. Many people were still awake. In the clutter of huts to the rear, someone picked at a guitar and sang. When the coyote yapping drifted under the bright moon, dogs back there challenged. Night insects chirped and sang. A night bird called from the lacy pepper trees off to the right as Hardisty and O'Meara crossed the open space with the long, narrow ladders.

Back there among the first grapevines, still hobbled by their chains, Juanito and Geoffrey Carruthers waited. Still deeper in the vineyard, bunches of tough buffalo ponies were being held while the owners fanned out, silent shadows with guns and knives. And on back in the orchards the same thing was happening. The night with all its little sounds and furtive movements was to Hardisty a bomb with fuse sputtering. The explosion was close.

Two more ladders were advancing to the house wall on the other side. Indians bellied to the earth were creeping closer to the guards at the front gate. Apaches did not fight at night. These Comanches and Kiowas would fight any time. But none of the planning had impressed Hardisty. Bluntly he had warned Juan Tomás about the Yellow Hairs. But Juan Tomás, in his way, had arrogance like Don Alfredo Delgado. Had a will which prevailed. Juan Tomás had raided Mexican *ranchos* before. He lacked respect for Mexican *rancheros*. He had killed them, taken their women, burned and looted their holdings.

But those had been ranches. Small holdings. Not great haciendas. This Hacienda of Our Lady of Sorrows with its mounted guards, its generations of invincibility, was something else.

Hardisty and O'Meara reached the high, thick adobe wall. O'Meara whispered, "This damn stinkin' cowhide. . . ."

Hardisty held silence as he placed the long, narrow ladder. It topped the wall by two feet. "Now the hide," he said. "And have your ladder ready."

The side poles of the narrow ladder bent as his weight mounted. And bent still more. Dangerously. He had been afraid of this. If the ladder snapped, he'd fall heavily.

71

The alarm might be given. The square of doubled cowhide across his shoulder was heavy and almost cut off breath with its rank, decaying stench. The ladder held.

He laid the doubled hide over cruelly jagged glass points plastered into the top of the wall. O'Meara had the other ladder ready. Hardisty hoisted it, lowered it inside the wall. Then, stepping gingerly across the cowhide, he got a foot on a top rung of the inside ladder, slid his weight over, and started the descent. O'Meara was coming up after him. If the burly Irishman's weight did not break either ladder, they might now have a chance of getting into the house. Beyond that, Hardisty did not plan. The rich, ripe smell of horse and cattle corrals, of wood smoke from smoldering cook fires, of long-discarded garbage and unwashed bodies had drifted on the slight breeze outside. Here, inside the high wall, the scent of flowers hung sweet and strong in the moonlight. Crickets were singing. A night bird trilled sweetly and was answered by another bird. House windows showed light.

O'Meara's broad shoulders came over the wall and started down like a monstrous, slow-swooping bat. They stood together among flowers which their feet trampled.

Hardisty muttered, "A door at the back, I guess. Servants go in and out that way. Should be one door unlocked." Gazing at O'Meara and down at himself, Hardisty added wryly, "We've looked better."

Their hair was long and tangled. Faces were dark with bristly beard stubble. Shirts were filthy and torn. Pants covered skin burned dark by the sun. Boots were pulled on over bare feet thickly callused. They had walked the long, endless days on the water wheels in bare feet, stripped nearly naked most of the time. Now gunbelts and revolvers were at their waists. They still wore the

72

rusted leg and wrist shackles. The lengths of rusty, broken chain were looped and tied around their ankles and right wrists.

O'Meara's sour chuckle was a soft rumble in his throat and thick neck. "First woman sees us'll scream."

They moved silently out of the flower beds, crossed a walk of packed, clean gravel which crunched slightly underfoot. Silently on grass, and through more flowers, skirting the towering pink wall of the house, they reached the back.

The first door Hardisty tried was bolted inside. He muttered an oath. The unpredictable Comanches were creeping closer. The quiet night was a delusion. The minutes were growing tauter, tauter. . . .

Off to the right was the white iron bench in the flower garden where Delgado had appreciated the scent of a flower while his men beat Hardisty for refusing to answer questions. The doorway from which Delgado had emerged was ahead. Hardisty went there. The wide, solid, hand-carved door was closed. The hammered iron latch gave beneath his thumb, and the unbarred door opened on gently creaking hinges.

Hardisty peered in, then stepped inside. This was a long passage ending in a moon-silvered inner patio. The house seemed immense when one moved through a portion of it like this. Part of the patio was in shadow. A flagstone walk ran around all four sides. Over the walk, all the way around, was a second floor balcony. Leafy vines reached up to the balcony railings. The scent of flowers was heavy in the cool night.

Voices were faintly audible in the back part of the house. A pan clanged there. A woman laughed. O'Meara touched Hardisty's shoulder. "Delgado?"

Hardisty pointed across the patio. Windows over there glowed softly with light. A door was open. A man's voice murmured. A woman spoke rapid, fluid Spanish. A second woman cut in. Another man's voice lifted.

Hardisty was slowly and silently following the flagstone walk around the patio, keeping over in the velvet-black shadows under the inner part of the balcony. The first softly-glowing window was framed inside by white lace curtains, open in the middle of the window.

When Hardisty looked cautiously through the window, the room inside was a long, high-ceilinged parlor. There were chairs and couches, curtains and darker draperies, framed paintings, two coal-oil lamps with large flowered-glass shades, and two silver candelabra in which candles were burning. And three women and two men.

One of the men was Don Alfredo de Leon y Delgado, long and lean, with the long, bony, humorless face of a Castilian aristocrat. The mouth was a stern gash, the chin lines had hatchet angles. The darker-hued skin suggested a liberal brush of Mexican-Indian rather than Moorish inheritance. His eyes had a dark, bored stare as he watched the young woman who had to be Ann Carruthers. Not a chance of mistake there.

The other two women, one evidently Delgado's wife, the other younger, were black-haired, dusky-skinned brunettes, obviously Mexican, and both plump. But the Carruthers girl was slender, with golden-tanned skin, thick brown hair that in the lamplight showed glints near reddish-gold as she moved her head. She looked young and earnest and was not smiling now as she spoke seriously. Hardisty heard only the murmur of her voice as he ducked under the window frame and went noiselessly to the open door. O'Meara was at his shoulder.

"This has to be fast," Hardisty breathed.

"And right," O'Meara whispered back with wry reminder. "It's for keeps. No time for mistakes or wasted minutes."

Hardisty nodded. Gun in hand he shouldered swiftly through the open doorway. His order in Spanish was brief and brusque.

"Quiet! All of you! No talk! Not a word!"

The older woman sucked breath in a gasp. The younger woman clapped a palm to her mouth, her eyes wide, staring. Ann Carruthers was startled. She sat rigid, half-turned in her chair, watching them, and for an instant her eyes had seemed to light with something close to hope as she saw that they were not Mexican. That look vanished as quickly as it came.

Delgado knew them instantly. His reaction was cold disdain. His warning was cold and measured. "This will not help. Get out before the guards shoot you, as they always do. Get out!" He moistened his lips. "It will please me to overlook this."

He was the breeding of generations of such dons on the Hacienda of Our Lady of Sorrows. Men who were never crossed. What they willed came to pass. What they desired was theirs. To speak was to have it happen. As boys it was so. As young men it wrapped them like a cloak of arrogant armor. In full middle age it was so habitual that it was taken for granted. All that ran through Hardisty's mind as he moved silently to the high-backed chair where Don Alfredo Delgado sat with stiff confidence and eyed him coldly.

Only fright, terror such as this man had never known would penetrate his arrogant armor. Hardisty sensed that and had the answer as he transferred the gun to his left hand and slowly shook out the rusty manacle chain attached to his right wrist. All the talk was still in Spanish.

"The keys, Delgado! To these irons! Quick!"

"You are given the warning, Gringo. The guards. . . ."

"Last chance!"

"You believe that I have fear of gringo dogs. . . ."

A pistol-whipping would easily beat the man down unconscious — and the only hope at getting the keys would vanish. There was a better way, a cruel way — and cruelty had been building in Hardisty each day on the water wheels, each lash of a guard's whip. It was the rusty wrist chain that met the coldly contemptuous will of Don Alfredo Delgado. The snake-like whisssh sounded again as the chain lashed in past the startled hand that was lifted. Into the face, across cheek and mouth of that coldly disdainful figure. And not gently.

The blow drove Delgado's head solidly against the carved high back of his chair. A cry, half-rage, half-groan of hurt and disbelief was driven from the man. Blood welled crimson on a torn lip.

Delgado gasped, "You will be. . . ."

The chain lashed in again, tearing a cheek this time, driving the man cowering down over the curved chair arm, his own arm lifted to protect his head.

The older woman sat frozen, her lips moving soundlessly. The younger man had the same frozen look of disbelief as O'Meara's gun — and the rusty chain on O'Meara's thick wrist — menaced him. But the Carruthers girl, pale and furious, came to her feet.

"You filthy brute! The man is helpless!"

"He's got armed men everywhere, protecting him," Hardisty said calmly. "You heard him. Now, sit down."

"I will not! Do you think I am afraid. . . ."

"Shut up!" Hardisty said coldly, and she was not used to talk like that, for her words ran out into silence while her eyes hated him. "Your brother," Hardisty said curtly, "is outside the house wall, chained like we were, wrists and ankles. I'm getting the keys for him. Now keep out of this."

"G-Geoffrey . . . ?"

"Yes!"

"You're lying! Geoffrey hasn't been here!"

O'Meara's biting warning cut through the room. "No time for this fancy talk!"

"I want her to get it through her silly head!" Hardisty said, tight-lipped. "She's got to understand, so she'll take orders fast." He spoke to the man in the high-backed chair, who had straightened a little. "Delgado! Is her brother here? Chained? On the water wheels? Or was! Speak fast!"

"I. . . ."

Ann Carruthers choked, "You could make him admit anything that way! How could Geoffrey. . . ."

Hardisty shut her off again. "Quiet, I told you! I want the keys to the prisoners' leg and wrist irons. He can stop all this with the keys."

The older woman gasped in Spanish, "Alfredo! For the love of God, before . . . before. . . ."

The younger woman was weeping. Hardisty wondered with some regret what she'd do when the Comanches burst in. He would have spared her that, but she had lived with the Delgado code in luxury and acceptance. Whatever happened now was a balancing of a long, long building account.

The young man was sitting on the edge of his chair in pale indecision. O'Meara used English matter-of-factly. "I'll kill this rooster if he tries what I think he'd like t' try. Ahhh! Savee English, *que no?* Sit back, then, an' stay healthy while you can!"

Hardisty lifted his own wrist chain. Don Alfredo Delgado cowered lower in his chair, his bent arm lifting higher to shield his bleeding face. His strangled words were really moaning defeat. "Across the patio. . . ."

"Watch here," Hardisty ordered O'Meara. He gestured with the gun. "Run, Delgado!"

The man lurched unsteadily to his feet and started to the door. The slashing chain across his back beat him into a stumbling run. It must have been the first time in his life that fright and pain had whipped him on. He ran across the flower-scented patio through bright moonlight and darker shadows and burst through a doorway.

They had entered a large bedroom dimly lit by a small glass lantern. Sobbing for breath in emotion that was out of control, Delgado clawed open the top drawer of a high chest of drawers. Fumbling inside he brought out a large ring filled with keys. His hand was shaking as he offered the ring.

Somewhere beyond the walled house area a gunshot slapped the still night with sharpness and threat. Then a second shot. A third. An Indian had been discovered. A young Comanche had been too restless to wait. Whatever. Time was now in short moments until the screaming rush of a full attack.

"Delgado, I'll kill you if these are the wrong keys!"

"The prisoner keys!"

Hardisty held out his left wrist. "Unlock!"

He thought the man's shaking hands would be unable to do it. But a key was selected, thrust into a shackle; effort turned the rusted lock and the shackle fell open. The jerk of Hardisty's wrist sent the iron circlet bouncing, skidding across the floor. He transferred the gun to his left hand and held out the right wrist. The ankle irons took a different key but they opened, also. Hardisty snatched the key ring.

"Run back! *¡Andale!*"

Now more gunshots, whoops, yells, screams were slashing violence through the distant night. Most of it, Hardisty judged, was coming from the huts, brush ramadas, and pen corrals sprawling widely in the area behind the house. His prisoner, still bleeding and panting hoarsely, lurched back into the parlor where O'Meara watched the others.

"Got 'em," Hardisty said, holding up the keys. "It's started outside. Nothing we can do to stop it." He spoke shortly to Ann Carruthers. "Indians out there. Comanches. You've got one chance to see your brother and get away. Come along if you want it."

Delgado's plump, frightened wife was crossing herself again as O'Meara turned to the door. Swinging to follow, Hardisty's glance crossed Delgado's look. The tall, lean Mexican, face smeared with blood, was watching him with half-crazed venom which would be in the man until one of them was killed, Hardisty realized.

He had chain-whipped this man into whimpering, cowering submission. He had made him run, cringing, like one of his own whipped peons. And in front of his own household. The shame and hate would be in the man while he lived. But he probably wouldn't live long with the Comanches of Juan Tomás attacking outside.

Chapter Seven

Behind Hardisty in the long, dim passage from the patio to the back of the house, Ann Carruthers called with a catch of breath, "I'll ha-have to believe G-Geoffrey's out there!"

She was running also, following. Hardisty was deliberately keeping ahead of her. Time was too short, risks too great to lag and argue with a strange girl. He tossed back to her over a shoulder. "Keep up with us if you want your brother!" Nevertheless he dropped back to her side, conscious how slender, young, and disturbed she was. Already she was breathing hard from the fast run in long, entangling skirts and petticoats. He took her arm, helping her on.

Ann panted, "Mr. Winn won't know where I've gone!"

"Who?"

"Mr. Zeke Winn. He went out to the corrals — or said he was going there."

"Zeke Winn? That old mountain loafer wolf? What's he doing on this hacienda?"

"G-guiding me."

"If he's out back, he's dead now, or will be unless he finds a hole quick. Forget him. If any man can take care of himself, Zeke Winn can."

O'Meara opened the rear door of the passage, shouldered out into the moonlight, revolver muzzle seeking trouble.

"Still clear," he called back and ran to the right, toward the ladder they had left against the wall.

Hardisty steered the girl that way. Beyond the fretwork of pepper tree foliage toward the back, beyond the high rear wall of the house grounds, the silver moonlight was smeared with the rising crimson glare of new fires. The huge, outlying haystacks first, Hardisty guessed from the fountaining sparks shooting toward the stars. There was much to burn back there. Even the brush ramadas chinked with mud would blaze, and all of it would give the red, terrifying glare the Comanches needed for their attack.

Ann Carruthers looked toward the fires as they ran. She made no comment. A small splinter of admiration touched Hardisty. In danger visibly getting worse, she was not showing panic.

Shouts, then gunshots broke out at the front gates as they ran past the corner of the house and out over flower beds toward the wall. In moonlight and reflected fire glare, Hardisty saw that the massive front gates were closed and barred. Evidently the first warning shots out back had alarmed the guards and given them time to close the gates. The Comanche attack should have come there first. Once the big house was taken, all the hacienda was vulnerable. Now the gates were barred. Indians evidently were on the outside and the gate guards were trading shots with them.

The narrow ladder was still there, bending, trembling under O'Meara's climbing weight. But it held as it had before. O'Meara was halfway up when a shout at the front gate was followed by the muzzle blink of a rifle shot and a curse from O'Meara as a bullet knocked bits

81

off the wall beyond him and glanced shrilly off into the night.

"Stay behind me!" Hardisty ordered the girl. He weighed the revolver in his hand against two rifles at least inside the gate, and used words instead, shouting vituperation like any peon of the corrals. *"¡Hijo de puta!* Kill Indians, not *compadres! ¡Picarón! ¡Cabrón!"*

Back came a shout, "By the four wounds, make known, thou goats! Without help, we die!"

"¡Con Dios!"

O'Meara looked over the wall and called, "Send 'er up."

"Can you climb that?" Hardisty threw at her.

She was already at the ladder. "I'm not helpless." Long skirts, petticoats and all she climbed more nimbly than O'Meara had. And gained another notch in Hardisty's esteem.

O'Meara had straddled the folded green cowhide which covered the jagged glass on top of the wall. He waited on the other side, gave her curt directions and descended. Ann Carruthers sat lightly on the folds of fresh hide, brought her legs and long skirt up neatly and over, and fumbled only a moment finding a top rung on the outside ladder.

As soon as her weight was off the inside ladder, Hardisty started up. He was nearing the top when shouts just back of the house warned of danger. A gun fired, then another. Bullets smashed into the wall by the ladder, driving bits of hard plaster against his legs. The ladder bowed dangerously under the drive of his climb. He was a full close target to several guns and, when he reached the green cowhide, he threw himself across with searching bullets dully smacking the wall even closer.

The girl was still on the ladder when his foot thrust

down, exploring. He felt her go off, and got his weight on a ladder rung and ducked down behind the protection of the top of the wall. Too close. His last look through the moonlight and fire glare had sighted a man with a yellow-haired vest running past the corner of the house toward the wall, shooting as he ran. More of the Yellow Hair guards evidently were inside the wall and had almost trapped O'Meara, himself, and Ann Carruthers. And the thought of what Don Alfredo Delgado would have ordered, if he and O'Meara had been dragged back to the house as prisoners, brought a cold prickle of danger to the back of Hardisty's neck. That venomous Mexican don was capable of ordering them flayed alive while Indians were at his gates. And it had been close. Close.

O'Meara's warning met him before he reached the ground. "Here's Juan Tomás! Hell's bustin' out all over the place, an' he waits here for them keys!"

Seven Indians were near the foot of the ladder, most of them wearing only breech-clouts and war paint. Hide covers were off their painted war shields. Dried scalps hung from war lances. The bold stripes of white, red, yellow and black paint gave them a hideous, sinister air. Hardisty had to remind himself that Juan Tomás was half-white, his thinking, in some ways, near that of a white man.

"You have keys, Hardisty?"

"Yes."

"This woman wife?"

"Yes."

Ann Carruthers gulped, "W-what did he s-say?"

"Quiet, or I'll beat you!" Hardisty warned in harsh anger. "This is man-business! Life or death! Understand?"

"You beat . . . she your woman," Juan Tomás conceded.

83

Hardisty hoped she understood enough to keep silent. He should have explained how it would have to be if she escaped. Matter-of-fact he had forgotten that her safety lay in being his wife before these woman-hungry Comanches.

He held up the keys. "Are Juanito and Carruthers where we left them?"

"*Si*," said Juan Tomás. "I go, too." He lifted his voice, giving rapid orders in grunt-click Comanche.

A breech-clouted, painted warrior ran toward the rear. Another ran toward the front. A third was climbing the ladder at Hardisty's elbow. He reached the top and looked over the wall — and guns blasted on the other side. The Indian's explosive grunt followed the sodden strike of a bullet into flesh and bone. He collapsed out from the ladder and struck the ground heavily and inertly, bouncing, rolling to Ann Carruther's feet. In the bright moonlight, the back of his head was blown out. Blood still poured forth.

Her strangled cry of horror was involuntary as she backed into the protective circle of Hardisty's arm.

"Easy, easy," he told her, and could feel horror stiffening her muscles. He told Juan Tomás, "Yellow Hairs are inside there now. They were shooting at me when I climbed over the wall. And they weren't there when we came out of the house."

Juan Tomás gave orders in Comanche, then, in English, to them, "You bring keys."

This, Hardisty thought, marked the man's feeling toward his son. Here, now, at the height of a huge raid deep in Mexico, Juan Tomás was taking time to see that his son was freed. And Hardisty sensed again that their own safety might be in the balance. What would happen if Juanito were not freed? That was possible. Delgado

84

was a man used to calculated trickery. He'd know well enough that the keys could only be tested against shackles under their eyes at the moment.

As they moved away from the wall, the lurid horror off to the left was becoming fully visible. Huge haystacks had been fired first. They were swirling masses of flame. Mushrooming columns of smoke carried up chunks of fire and leaping curtains of sparks. Brush huts and wooden sheds were blazing. And through the smoke and sparks and red glare the peon men, women, and children were running helplessly.

Guns were forbidden them. The Yellow Hairs carried the only guns on the hacienda. Now knives and makeshift clubs and panicked flight were the only protection against breech-clouted figures stabbing with short war lances, killing with rifles and revolvers, axing, knifing, scalping in running frenzies of attack.

Hardisty had more or less ignored the fort-like barracks of the Yellow Hairs against the wall of the big house. The swift appearance of armed guards inside the house wall, the visible lack of protection for the peons showed how the hacienda was organized. The house and barracks of the guards were one unit, forted and armed. Those who lived outside that fortress line took their chances. They were replaceable. Easily. But to get at the Yellow Hairs and the occupants of the house, attackers needed a cleverly planned strike at weak points. And the Comanches had not reasoned all that out, and followed it.

They were crossing to the vineyard through open moonlight. Gunshots opened up behind them. The sound of giant bees droned close. Hardisty guided the girl in front of him and looked back.

"Shooting at us through the gun ports in the wall."

O'Meara was contemptuous. "They couldn't hit a haystack this far away. Not at night. Wonder why they keep wastin' catridges on us."

"Delgado probably ordered it."

"Likely. He'd near let the Comanch's in if he could gun us down for those dimples you put in his face."

"I'm beginning to wonder if we've seen the last of Delgado."

"Not if he c'n find us! He won't forget. Not that'n. Last thing he does in this life'll be to get us if he can!"

"I think that, too."

"If he ain't kilt tonight, we're in trouble."

"I'm beginning to doubt that he will be killed," Hardisty said.

An owl hooted loudly and carelessly in the first grape vines just ahead. Gunfire was still reaching after them. The sharp snap and leafy slash of bullets cutting through the vines was audible as they pushed in out of sight. Chains jingled and Juanito's voice said, "My father. . . ."

"Son. . . ."

"Where is Carruthers?" Hardisty asked.

"Here. Ann . . . ?"

"Jeff! Oh, Jeff! I couldn't believe it. Are you chained like . . . ? You are! Jeff! What happened?"

Geoffrey Carruthers was sitting on the ground between the vine rows. At the moment it meant nothing to Hardisty as he tried to find the key to Juanito's wrist shackles. Patches of moonlight among the vines helped. Then, abruptly, Juanito's wrists were free. Juan Tomás lingered while Hardisty knelt for the ankle irons.

O'Meara suddenly sounded worried.

"One of them bullets that missed us hit the Limey here. Thats why he's sittin' down."

The sister's panic burst from her this time. "Jeff, you didn't say you were hurt!"

"Stiff lip, Ann. These things happen."

"Let me. . . ."

"Not right now."

Juanito's ankle irons yielded to the key Hardisty located. When Hardisty came to his feet, Juan Tomás put a hand on his shoulder. "Friend," the Comanche said. For the moment, at least, he seemed to mean it. "Juanito give you horses, food. You stay fight tonight or go with woman." Then he was gone, a dark shadow whisking through the last screen of vines, running back through the moonlight to the fire glare and frenzy of the attack.

Hardisty went to his knees again by Carruthers, fumbling with the seemingly endless ritual of the keys. Ann Carruthers knelt on the other side of her brother. Some inner strength was holding her dry-eyed and outwardly calm against what was ahead.

"Where'd it hit?" Hardisty inquired.

"Ribs."

"Bleeding much?"

"No."

"Can you walk?"

"I . . . I think so. Knocked me groggy at first. Better now."

Wrist irons, then ankles irons yielded to the keys. Carruthers also was free. O'Meara's shackles followed, then Hardisty hurled the clinking key ring into the vineyard dirt, next to the hated irons, not knowing he would regret that later.

Juanito said, "You come. . . ."

"Lady," O'Meara said, "you follow Hardisty. I'll help your brother."

She obeyed. The young Comanche led them deeper into the vineyard to ponies concealed out of sight. In bunches, rein ropes held by guards, the ponies were bareback, with a single jaw rein. They looked undersized, scrawny, lacking bottom. Actually, they were tough horseflesh, making possible the long, grueling rides of the raiding Comanches. Juanito selected four ponies haphazardly.

"You wait here," he suggested, "then ride with us."

"Maybe," Hardisty said. "Right now I'll go with you. I want to see what's happening."

Juanito had taken a rifle from one of the pony guards. He spoke jerkily to Hardisty as they trotted through the moonlight toward the flames and screams, the whoops and gunshots.

"What you t'ink, Hard'sty?"

"Think about what?"

"Indian fight here . . . you t'ink good?"

"Your people haven't gotten inside that big wall around the house."

"No."

"I think it's too late now. I don't think they'll get in. And the fires now are only making Comanches good targets for the Yellow Hair guns."

"I t'ink so, too," Juanito said absently. "I t'ink dis not good."

Hardisty had wondered if he might not find a rifle and some cartridges. Off of a dead Indian possibly. Also he needed to know how the raid was going. Before they reached the first fires, he had seen enough. He turned back at a faster trot.

"This raid will fizzle out," he said jerkily to O'Meara and Carruthers, who was sitting down again. "The Yellow Hairs are forted up and potting Indians through rifle slits. The Indians can't get at them. They won't get in now. They'll have peon scalps, some peon women and children, and junk they've looted. And horses. And Juanito. But the hacienda won't be crippled. All the hacienda guns will be full of fight. Carruthers! Can you ride tonight? All night?"

"I . . . will it be that bad?"

"Delgado won't even be thinking of Indians," was Hardisty's guess. "He'll want us. O'Meara and me, especially. But all of us now, so there'll be no talk. We won't have many hours start."

"Where to? Paso del Norte and across the river?"

"That," said Hardisty, "is exactly where Delgado and his men will be certain we've headed. Any direction but Paso del Norte!"

Chapter Eight

The dusty, weather-scoured J.F. Bennet stagecoach from Paso del Norte, Mesilla, and Las Cruces reached Santa Fe on a comfortably cool late afternoon. Cool, that is, after the heat of Paso del Norte and Mesilla. The plaza at Santa Fe was seven thousand feet, almost a mile, higher than Paso del Norte. At the hotel stop on the southeast corner of the plaza, the bony little man with a ragged chin beard who climbed stiffly down from the stage was old Zeke Winn.

A man, among the watchers who had gathered, greeted him. Zeke Winn absently lifted a hand. He did not smile. The wrinkled, dark-parchment face looked older. The skinny frame seemed shrunken inside the ill-fitting salt-and-pepper suit. His question to the man who had greeted him was without anticipation.

"Where c'n I find Judge Bassett?"

"Ain't seen him in the hotel. Likely he's still over't the bank, trying for that last dollar in town."

Another bystander chuckled. "Likely he's got that last dollar already, or knows where 'tis. Colin never had flies on his eyes."

Zeke Winn walked over into the plaza. Another long wagon train off the Santa Fe trail had arrived within the last day or so. Huge, high-wheeled freight wagons cluttered the plaza and the narrow, dusty side streets. The walks were crowded again and the open-air monte games were running in daylight.

The bank was closed. Front window shades were drawn. But when Zeke Winn knocked loudly and kept knocking, he finally heard steps inside. The edge of the door shade was pulled back revealing the peering, stocky, white-haired figure of Judge Bassett. The banker's quick smile held anticipation as he unbolted the door.

"Zeke! When did you return?"

"Jes' crawled off the stage." Zeke Winn walked in without an answering smile. "Don't ask me if that Miss Carruthers come back, too. She didn't."

These two old friends had shared blankets when they were younger. Judge Colin Bassett could sense the moods of the bony little man. Now he closed and bolted the door again, and said quietly, "Come into the office, Zeke. We can talk there."

In a small, dusty office in the back corner of the banking room, Zeke Winn dropped into the armchair at a corner of the paper-cluttered roll top desk. He bit the end from a cigar Bassett handed him and drew the cigar alight from the flaring match Bassett offered.

"I'm a hell of a nurse-maid, Colin."

Bassett shook the match out and rolled it slowly between his fingers. "Don't tell me that little lady gave you the slip, Zeke."

"You c'n call it that. The Comanch's got her."

"What?" Bassett dropped the dead match, his mouth slightly open. "Comanches? They got Miss Carruthers?"

"Yep."

"Got her? Ann Carruthers?"

"You heerd me."

"Killed her? Don't you mean Apaches, Zeke?"

"Goddamnit, Colin! I know a Comanch' from an

91

Apach'! I said the Comanches got her. Maybe she's dead, mebbe she ain't. Better she is dead. You know what them war bucks do to a woman. Pass 'er around the ring 'til she's dead. If there's any life left in 'er, most likely they'll bash 'er head in."

"I know. . . ." Judge Bassett looked sick. "That girl. . . ." He took a cigar from the box on the desk, regarded it sightlessly, and hurled it to the floor. "Tell me, Zeke. . . ."

"I'll get it all out while I'm here. First. You didn't get cute with a ol' has-been like me, Colin? You didn't send another man along on this business?"

"I don't even know what you're talkin' about."

"Jack Cultus is who I'm talkin' about."

"That. . . ." Colin Bassett flapped an irritated, negative hand. "I run a bank, Zeke, and try not to deal with men like Cultus. Gunmen, killers, rascals like Cultus, only mean trouble for a bank."

"Jack Cultus climbed on the southbound stage at the La Bajada stop. Lookin' back, I can see that he rode a hoss nigh into a founder to catch that stage. All the way from Santa Fe. So he wanted bad to be on the same stage I was on an' the little lady was on. At the time it didn't mean nothin', save I had to sit with a skunk day after day. Wasn't 'til Mesilla I found out he was ahead of me tryin' to get track of the girl's brother." Zeke Winn told what had happened. "Soon as he cut the brother's sign, he sold out of Mesilla for Paso del Norte, an' then on to Azul, in Mexico, cold-trackin' the brother."

Bassett was shaking his head, frowning. "I can't guess why. I'd swear Geoffrey Carruthers never laid eyes on Cultus. Or heard about him, for that matter."

"It couldn't have been some trouble between 'em?"

"I'm positive not."

92

"Clears it up some, then. Someone sent Cultus hell-bent after the girl after she left Santa Fe."

"I'm the only one knew she was going, Zeke."

"Then someone seen her leavin' on the stage. That minute he got the idea she'd best be followed, an' sent Cultus fast after the stage, to catch it at the La Bajada stop."

"That does make some sense."

"Not enough," Zeke Winn said bluntly. "Who knew the brother was gone? An' might have an idea where he went? And who give a damn about it anyway? Who'd it help? Who'd it hurt if the brother was tracked down?"

"Zeke, you're asking questions I can't answer. But I can suggest this: when people from distant England pour money into developing a great ranch, like the Vuelta Grant is planned to become, many lives are affected."

"What you're tryin' to say, Colin, is that money is honey."

"In a way."

"And draws flies an' bees, bears an' men, an' skunks."

"Exactly."

"So the brother was important."

"The sister is half-owner."

"Cultus was trackin' the brother," Zeke reminded dryly. "And the brother hired a hoss at Azul and headed out east to a big hacienda owned by a Mexican named Don Alfredo Delgado."

"Hell's howling pups!" Colin Bassett blurted. "That'd be the Delgado spread . . . Hacienda of Our Lady of Sorrows! Famous all over northern Mexico."

"Un-huh."

"And that Delgado family owned the Vuelta Grant, and lost it in court to Simon Roddan who sold the Vuelta to Geoffrey and Ann Carruthers. Now you say Carruthers

93

went into old Mexico, to the Delgado hacienda?"

"I say he headed that way. I heerd Delgado tell the girl that her brother never reached the hacienda. The hoss he rented drifted back to Azul a few days later. We already knew that. They never had found the rider."

"What about Jack Cultus?"

"He rode to the hacienda. Ahead of us. Got the same story an' started back to Azul. We missed him. Never did sight him after leavin' Mesilla."

"I see. Let me get this straight, Zeke. You reached the hacienda with Miss Carruthers, I gather. And inquired about her brother. So she was safe there."

"I'd have swore so," said Zeke Winn glumly. "They dug out the deep sheepskin. Treated the little lady like she was fam'ly. Cut it high on the hog for ol' Zeke, too, on account I was with her. The fancy eatin' and gabblin' talk stuffed my craw. I went out back to the corrals to talk with the *pelados*. If there was back-of-the-hand talk about a gringo shot off his hoss between the hacienda and Azul, a few pesos for a mescal drunk might bring it out."

"And did it?" Judge Bassett inquired with close interest.

"Nobody would admit knowin' a thing. They wouldn't even take my pesos . . . which was as good as admittin' they knew somethin'. They knew plenty, an' was afraid to say so."

"You think, Zeke, they knew who had killed Geoffrey Carruthers?"

"I ain't sure what I think . . . an' the men I was talkin' to . . . the men who knowed somethin', I was sure . . . won't never tell now, 'cause they're dead."

"All of them?"

Zeke Winn nodded. He was matter-of-fact.

94

"I went for a walk in the moonlight, puzzlin' it over. And it struck me the coyotes an' owls was mighty busy. I scouted out from there, doin' some owl talk meself, an' I coaxed out the damndest war-painted Comanch' I ever seen. He looked big as a loblolly pine. Dunno who was the most surprised . . . him, I guess, because I shot him afore he got his rifle unlimbered. An' like it was a signal, it set off one hell of a Comanch' raid. They was everywhere, all over the place. The moon was full . . . reglar Comanch' Moon . . . and they fired the haystacks when that first shot set everything off. It made enough light for a Bible-reading, an' it looked like Indians was coming out of the tree bark and rocks. Everywhere. Had me cut off from the house. I sold out of there with the dead 'uns rifle while I still had hair."

"Were the Delgados killed also?"

"They had a set-up that was planned to fight off Indian raids. Armed guards lived in a kind of fort-barracks behind the house wall, where they could get into the house fast. There's a high wall around the house. Gun slits everywhere. An' the *pelados* an' their families livin' out in the open like free bait to keep the Indians busy while the house got organized. I laid off in the night watchin' Comanch's burnin' an' killin' an' scalpin' while the hell was bein' shot out of 'em by the forted-up rifles. When they quit finally, they'd give up tryin' to get into the big house. And all they had was scalps, prisoners, junk from the peon huts, and what hacienda hosses was in close. When mornin' came, wasn't anything in the open but bodies, burned shacks an' sheds, an' what few peons had managed to run fast enough an' far enough to hide. An' they was still cryin' an' prayin'."

"That sounds as if the Indians did not get into the main house."

Zeke Winn made a futile gesture with his cigar. "They didn't. But Miss Carruthers had gone out for a walk, same as I did. Delgado himself told me. Her body wasn't found, so she was alive when some buck grabbed her. Twelve hours later if she was still alive, there ain't no doubt she wanted to be dead."

Judge Bassett winced and pushed uneasy fingers through his shock of white hair. "These things are always horrible. But when they happen to someone we know. . . ."

Old Zeke said fiercely, "I was supposed to be watchin' over her. I damn near went on my knees askin' Delgado to let me ride with the first guards that went out. Our two hosses had been stole by the Indians. Delgado claimed they hadn't been able to chouse up enough fresh hosses to give me one. Late that day he had an old buggy mare turned over to me with polite orders to ride back to Azul. Any word about Miss Carruthers would be sent on." Old Zeke was bitter. "Them Comanch's was smokin' back to Texas with a twelve hour start. A man on a fast hoss probably couldn't have caught 'em. And lookin' all over north Mexico for a girl's body didn't promise much."

"Zeke, you're not being blamed for a thing."

"The hell I ain't. I'm blamin' myself. Shoulda' been with her every step outside that house at night."

"You weren't there when she went out. You couldn't have known she meant to leave the house after dark."

"I should have knowed."

"Too hard on yourself; too hard." Judge Bassett fell silent before he murmured, "Brother and sister. Both gone."

"Seems so," Zeke Winn assented. "While I was waitin' in Azul for word that never came from Delgado, I scouted back along the hacienda road for any sign of the brother.

Wasn't any. Too much time had passed."

"What did this Jack Cultus do?"

"Took a stage south from Azul. Lookin' for sign of the brother down Chihuahua way, I reckon."

"I haven't noticed Cultus back in Santa Fe." The Judge was in an absent mood again. He reached for another cigar. This time he bit the end off, spat it aside, and lighted it. He was grave when he finally spoke.

"The Vuelta Ranch that Geoffrey and Ann Carruthers own is an immense, valuable property. A small fortune has been spent already in taking a wild, unsettled Spanish grant and getting a working ranch started. And now we think both owners are dead."

"The Comanch' don't kill every woman," Zeke said gloomily. "Not the young ones. If she ain't passed over the prairie to all the bucks, one man'll take her for a slave."

Judge Bassett again winced at the thought.

"That only complicates the situation, Zeke. Without legal proof of death, the ranch still officially belongs to Geoffrey and Ann Carruthers."

Zeke Winn's shrewd comprehension showed on his dark, wrinkled face. "They won't own much after the news gets out," Zeke hazarded.

Colin Bassett slapped the desk.

"Exactly! The ranch can't be sold. Legally it must be held as it is. But when word gets out that the owners have vanished, and are probably dead, that ranch will be like a fat range cow with a broken leg. Every coyote and wolf in the Territory will move in for easy meat." Bassett turned a speculative gaze on the bony old figure sitting at the corner of his desk. "Have you mentioned any of this to anyone this side of the Delgado hacienda?"

97

"I ain't a loose mouth."

"Then we're the only two who know it."

"Jack Cultus knows about the brother. If Cultus goes back to the hacienda, he'll hear about the sister." Zeke Winn squinted. "Whoever sent Cultus after the brother, has ideas about something."

"If the real facts are kept quiet, there will be time to find the man and his motive. Miss Carruthers left me written instructions. In case she dropped out of sight and her brother had not reappeared, the bank is to have the Vuelta continue as is. In sixty days, the English branch of the family is to be notified, and the bank will wait for further instructions."

Zeke Winn's snort was eloquent.

"A ranch crew ain't fools. Not all the men. When owners don't show up for months, they guess somethin's wrong."

"Not," said Bassett, "if a trip were made, say to England. That can be arranged, I think, with proper care that no one else learns what we know." Bassett's glance turned speculative again. "And then, Zeke, if you could drift around the Vuelta and keep me informed. . . ."

"No!" Zeke Winn said quickly, flatly and coolly. "Got my own whittlin' to do now. You get some'n else to spy for you."

"I need you!"

Zeke Winn stood up. Shrunken, bony in the wrinkled salt-and-pepper suit, there was an odd dignity and force about him.

"Them Comanches headed back up to Texas. A bunch that big took captives along, women, kids. Comanches and Kiowas have been raidin' everywhere. They'll have stolen cattle and hosses, and the Comancheros from New Mexico will be on the plains tradin' with 'em. One of

98

them captives might be our little lady. I'm goin' with the Comancheros. Least I can do is find her, or news that she's alive or dead."

Chapter Nine

The red glare of burning haystacks and outbuildings, the sharp wham and slap of gunfire, whoops, cries, screams, still smeared and tore the night as Hardisty made his decision in the green rows of the large vineyard.

"We'll leave now and get as far as we can before dawn." His question to Ann Carruthers was brief. "Can you ride?"

Her hostility lurked close under the surface.

"I've ridden all my life. But with a proper saddle." She glanced at the four Indian ponies which had been turned over to them. O'Meara was holding the jaw reins, more or less ignoring her as he looked warily about. "These horses haven't any saddles."

"They're Indian war ponies, ma'am, all we have," Hardisty said with thin patience. "You'll ride bareback like a man."

"But I can't be expected. . . ."

He cut her short, deliberately brusque. "Then stay behind and take your chances."

"You know I wouldn't leave my brother! Must you be a . . . a. . . ."

". . . a dirty brute," Hardisty finished dryly for her. "I'm dirty and brutal and if I save your life, I save mine, too, which is all I'm interested in."

"Ann! Keep your temper," Geoffrey Carruthers said

thinly. "Can't you see none of us is safe until we're across the border? Far across. Hardisty is trying to get us there."

Hardisty had turned his back. "Help her on a pony, O'Meara, if she needs it. I'll see to Carruthers."

He had a reason for helping the Englishman. The new white manta cloth peon's shirt and pants that had been given to Carruthers when he was taken into the house showed only a hand-sized patch of blood on the right side, at the lower ribs. It could mean a slight nick by a bullet, or something far different.

"Take my hand," Hardisty said. When he pulled Carruthers up, the hand felt sweaty, hot. "How's your side?"

"As soon as I'm on a horse. . . ."

Hardisty lifted the bottom of the loose shirt and saw in the moonlight the small dark hole going in. That was not a shallow, glancing wound. The bullet had gone in deeply; the wound had partially closed; the bleeding was inside. That was the moment Hardisty suspected he was looking at a dying man. He guessed that Carruthers had known it almost from the impact of the bullet.

The sister could hear what was said. Carruthers sucked a deep slow breath and said quietly, "Help me on the horse. Important thing is to get Ann far and fast from here. To keep riding no matter what. . . ."

It was useless, Hardisty knew, to argue with a dying man whose only concern was for his sister's safety. Staying here through the night with Carruthers would not help the man much, and would be disastrous for the rest of them.

"We'll ride easy," Hardisty said quietly. "It's a long time until daylight. We can get a long start." He helped Carruthers on a pony. "I'll lead off to the end of the vineyard. Just follow easy."

What really passed between them was unspoken but

understood. Carruthers would not have been left there. They all would have waited with him. So a dying man was forcing himself to ride so that they could ride, also.

Hardisty gave scant attention to the girl. With or without O'Meara's help, she was awkwardly astride her bareback pony. And from now on her moods would get short shrift, Hardisty reflected, as he followed the vineyard rows well ahead of the others.

Far over to the left he heard the crashing of horses being driven through the vineyard by whooping, yelling Indians. And heard, even closer, the sharp snap and crackle of vines as a lone rider forced a fast way through, angling toward him.

The rider seemed to be on a fractious horse. Advancing rushes swung sharply left, then right. Then wheeled back. Then reversed and came crashing on again. Hardisty could see the moonlight glinting on a waving lance head and white-banded head feathers on the bobbing, twisting head of the horse as it zigzagged and wheeled among the vines.

Suddenly what was happening became clear. Something was fleeing through the masking vines, dodging, doubling back, vanishing, then being sighted again by the Indian. It had to be human. Only that would draw stubbornly eager pursuit in the midst of a fiery, bloody raid. Someone hiding in the vineyard had been flushed into flight by the crashing horse herd, and now was being ridden down for death or capture. If Hardisty had stopped to reason, he would have ridden on. Instead he yanked the pony left toward the approaching rider, and in a half-dozen yards almost rode down the victim.

A dark figure, stooped and scuttling, flung itself rustling and panting through the grape vines. It sighted Hardisty's horse almost overhead and straightened, swaying back with a stifled cry.

Still on impulse, Hardisty grabbed an up-flung arm and with a mighty haul manhandled the figure up before him on the horse. His arm went around the convulsively panting figure of a girl whose breasts were firm and whose knee-length shift was plastered to her thin figure by streaming sweat. She was instinctively fighting him, writhing, clawing, kicking. Long black hair was a matted tangle around her face and shoulders. Her hair bunched across Hardisty's face, strong with woman smell, and through the tangle across her own face came little convulsive, panting, animal-like sounds.

In Spanish, Hardisty rasped angrily, "Quiet, you little she-devil! I'm trying to help you!"

The other rider almost crashed into them. He pulled up violently, lance lifted threateningly. Hardisty pulled the revolver Juan Tomás had given him.

In bad, halting Spanish, the Indian said harshly, "Woman me!"

Hardisty said roughly in better Spanish, "My woman, ask Juan Tomás!"

It didn't work. This one was in a woman-hungry rage. The lance flashed back to spear one or both of them. Without time to argue or think, Hardisty shot!

The booming, livid-spitting shot struck the painted belly square center, driving the Indian spinning off. Hardisty yanked his own horse swiftly around and grabbed the rein of the other horse.

The girl had been shocked motionless by the gun blast so close to her face. Her slender figure, molded rigidly against Hardisty while her palms covered her ears and she gazed without seeming comprehension at the riderless horse. Hardisty's left arm held her and the rein of his own horse. The other hand held his revolver and the rein of the Indian's pony while Hardisty stared off through the moonlight at the fast receding bunch of horses.

No rider there seemed to be turning back. The night behind them where the flames leaped and crackled was a bedlam of gunshots. One more shot probably meant little in the tumult.

O'Meara had kicked his pony into a run that brought him up ahead of the others.

"I had to shoot that Indian off his horse," Hardisty said calmly. "See if he's dead. If he has a gun, get it."

O'Meara was already down, pushing back grape vines, holding his pony's rein as he knelt by the slack figure. "He won't get any deader. Got a revolver an' belt with a few cartridges. What happened?" O'Meara groaned. "Another female? Is that what you've got an armful of?"

"Just a child," said Hardisty hastily. He lifted her upright before him on the horse as Ann Carruthers and her brother reached them. "She was hiding in the vineyard, I guess, and was driven out when the horses were running through. She was darting and dodging through the vines. He'd have had her in another minute or so." In Spanish he asked the girl, "Your name, little one?"

"Rosa Lopez." She had caught her breath and pushed and shaken the mass of black hair off her face. "I am your woman now, no?" she said over her shoulder. "You kill for me. I don't fight you, *Señor Gringo.*"

Ann Carruthers said, "A little child, I believe you said?"

Hardisty saw the grin which touched O'Meara's face. His own heavily stubbled face was heating in the moonlight. "Rosa, can you ride a horse?"

She relaxed against him like a trusting kitten. "I like much better this way, *Señor Gringo.*"

She had an elfin young profile framed by the tangled black hair, but when Hardisty saw the grin spreading on O'Meara's face he said brusquely, "Rosa, do you want to go with the Indians?"

"Sweet mother of God, no!"

"Do you want to go with us?"

"I am your woman now, *Señor Gringo*."

"Get on that horse and and stay with the lady."

He eased her to the ground and watched her take the rein from O'Meara with casual ease. She gripped a handful of mane and flipped up on the pony's bare back in one lithe movement. In the bright moonlight the short, white manta cloth dress molded damply to her slender figure. She had a lithe, startlingly mature look as she sat lightly, erectly on the horse.

O'Meara mounted again and Hardisty shifted into English. "If the Indians find this dead one, they may think he was shot nearer the house and got this far before he fell off."

"An' if they don't?"

"Could be bad," Hardisty admitted. "Juan Tomás and Juanito and any Indians who'll obey them are the only help we'll get in Mexico. If the Comanches start hunting us, too, I don't think we'll make it!"

"No grub; no water. Not even a rifle. Two women. . . ."

"I've been thinking. The cook shack at the water wheels. Grub there!"

"If it ain't been stole."

"The Indians who came for Juanito were starting a raid. They've been too busy since."

"I never thought I'd want to see those damn wheels again."

Chapter Ten

The two huge water wheels loomed dark, motionless in the moonlight. Distance softened the gunshots and yells of the raid. The fierce watch dogs lay where they had been lanced by the Indians. Moonlight through the gaping doorway of the prisoners' hut fell like a silvery benediction over Big Luis, the guard. He had not moved since O'Meara's rigid fingers had released his throat.

Rosa Lopez, holding the single rein of her pony, peered past Hardisty's elbow. "*El Azote* — The Whip," she said calmly in Spanish. "Dead, no?"

"Dead, and a young girl shouldn't be looking at such things."

"*Señor Gringo*, I am eighteen years . . . a woman. Your woman. Have I the soft belly that cannot see dogs without *vomito*?"

"You are not my woman," Hardisty said hastily. "*Señor* O'Meara will show you where the food was. Help there."

He lighted the lantern Big Luis had dropped. The shackled peons were gone, in terror evidently, shuffling, hobbling off into the night, cringing, hiding breathlessly now.

Geoffrey Carruthers had slipped off his horse and was sitting with his back against the adobe wall of the guards shack. The sister, asking questions, was getting for the first time, Hardisty guessed, some idea of what it had meant to be a shackled prisoner on the huge water wheels. This was — and there was irony in it — the one possible spot on the hacienda they could get help tonight. There was a battered tin canteen and small clay *ollas* with rawhide slings. In the cook hut was pinole, parched corn made into meal with sugar mixed in. There were wrinkled, black sheets of *carne seca,* the sun-jerked meat. And cold corn tortillas, coffee, black beans, two dark, flat rounds of goat cheese. And empty cloth sacks, most of them dirty from being used for cook aprons and towels.

Working fast, helped by both girls, sacks were stuffed with food and tied together into crude cloth saddlebags. The single canteen and small clay *ollas* were filled with water from the lagoon. Blankets were taken from the guards' shack. O'Meara's gusty humor was briefly catching as they mounted to ride off.

"We've got a chance now if them yellow-vested hacienda guards don't sight us."

They rode east toward the foothills and mountains which formed a haze-mantled line in daylight. Behind them, the flames had vented their first fury and stained the night less and less.

The racket of the raid died away. The night quieted into a false peace. These were the first miles of open grazing land. The unshod ponies moved quietly. They should have been trotting, loping. Instead, the long easy walk was at Hardisty's order.

Ann Carruthers rode beside her wounded brother. When Hardisty dropped back to see how the man was doing, she spoke of Don Alfredo Delgado with biting anger.

"I could not suspect that anything like those water wheels and chained prisoners would be possible among civilized people."

"They have chain gangs in the United States. Men living in chains, working in chains. Probably have them in England, also."

"The law does that."

"Here, Delgado is the law. He can order a peon whipped to death. Have a man shot. He's the *patrón*."

"He is horrible. Geoffrey tells me you discovered valuable ore and told this man Delgado about it. And he had chains put on you."

"It was bonanza silver, in the mountains east of here, where we're heading." Hardisty smiled thinly in the moonlight. "I had sense enough to cover traces of the ore outcrop before I took samples to Delgado. They were so rich the silver could be smelted out with a campfire. But I was in Mexico without much money and no influence. This could be a great fortune. It was best to work with a powerful man like Delgado.

"I didn't know him then. I offered him half. He decided to take it all with the claim he owned the land. He offered to hire me to work the mine for him. When I wouldn't show him the bonanza vein, he decided a few weeks on the water wheels would change my mind." Hardisty's chuckle was dry. "His greed for that bonanza silver might have broken him before I broke, but the raid tonight settled all that."

"My brother says that Mr. O'Meara struck one of the Delgado men. . . ."

"The oldest son. O'Meara was traveling north to the border on a fine stallion he'd won in a card game. At a little plaza called Esmeralda, south of here, the young Delgado, with four hacienda guards along, saw O'Meara's stallion and wanted to buy it. For about half its real value. When O'Meara laughed at him, young Delgado lost his temper. O'Meara hit him and broke his nose. One of the guards slugged O'Meara with a gun barrel. They brought O'Meara in an ox cart to the water wheels as a lesson to other men who might want to hit Delgado. And young Delgado got the stallion for nothing."

"Barbaric!"

"Logical . . . to a Delgado."

Ann Carruthers blazed under her breath, "I don't like a Mexico that allows their kind to exist!"

She was young, emotional, with sensitive imagination and temper which provocation could send flaring. Hardisty was not many years older. But on the slow-turning water wheels where no mercy was shown temper or weakness, he had learned the ancient lesson that when muscles faltered, the spirit within could still fight on. But when the spirit faltered, all strength vanished. O'Meara, the wild black Irishman, twelve years older than Hardisty, had never learned that furious temper was only a waste, a weakness.

Tonight death had brushed them closely. Now they had a chance to live. Possibly, even Geoffrey Carruthers had a chance to live. Riding in pallid silence, Carruthers seemed to be holding strength. He was calm when he spoke.

"Ann, I want to talk to Hardisty alone. Would you mind?"

Her quick alarm was visible and audible.

"Jeff. Are you worse?"

"No. But there's quite a bit to discuss with Hardisty. We have to plan, y'know."

Halfway disbelieving him, she put her horse forward where young Rosa Lopez was silently following the burly O'Meara. Ann was riding astride without further argument, her long skirts pushed down as far as possible.

There was much about her that was admirable, Hardisty was forced to admit.

Carruthers's question was quiet.

"D'you really believe there's a chance of getting Ann across the Rio Grande to safety?"

This was a time for candor and truth.

"I don't know," Hardisty admitted. "If Delgado sends the Yellow Hairs after us . . . and he will if he thinks there's a chance of getting at us . . . and they find us this side of the river, or even some distance on the other side, we won't have much chance. No rifles, no reserve of ammunition for even a try at standing them off.

"On the other hand," Hardisty continued bluntly, "if we can join Juan Tomás and his men as they head to the Rio Grande and on north, and stay with them. . . ."

"They'll be traveling fast?"

"I suppose so."

"And I couldn't keep up?"

"You know how you feel. I don't."

"I can keep on this way . . . slow."

"How far? How long without rest?"

They were brutal questions which needed asking and answering. And yet how brutal could one man be to a man who carried a bullet inside?

"I won't hold the rest of you back," Carruthers said evenly. "But while we're talking, I want to say that on those water wheels a man comes through more clearly in days and weeks than in years, otherwise."

"I agree."

"Ann is still a young girl, not too experienced. The Vuelta is a large undertaking, a heavy responsibility. All that will increase."

"You've made it sound so."

"If I could get back to the ranch with Ann, the future

110

would be reasonably secure. Never another foolish adventure like crossing the border to investigate cheap cattle and horses."

"That," Hardisty made a guess, "isn't what you're trying to say."

Carruthers's voice was quietly thoughtful, touched with introspection.

"I have a bad habit of keeping my real thoughts to myself. Not intentional secrecy, but you can see what a frightful mess it can make. The Vuelta only has a foreman in charge now. If Ann should return alone, she would face a heavy burden. Your American West is a man's world."

"You're still not saying what you think," Hardisty guessed again, dryly.

"Very well. If Ann should be alone and need help, will you help her?"

"I'm doing my best now."

"Help her with the Vuelta, I mean."

"If she should want my help; if it would be worth anything to her. But," said Hardisty, humor touching his words, "I'll guess she'll only want me to vanish, fast and forever."

"Dont judge Ann by her emotion tonight. Too much has happened to her too fast. I'll talk to her further. And about the Vuelta. . . . ?"

"Yes?"

Off in the south a coyote howled and broke into yapping clamor. Answers still farther away reached to the stars. Not Indians, Hardisty decided. Insects were singing and chirping. The silver moon globe floated high and bright. Violence and death seemed distant and unreal. As unreal as Hardisty's belief that he was talking to a dying man, who now spoke earnestly.

"I want you to understand. You've probably guessed that I'm a younger son. But not a blacksheep or outcast. The family has given me affection and help beyond my deserving. I had my chance to go out into the world and build, like those who went before me. Does that make sense to you?"

"Are you trying to say that your older brother inherited a large estate?"

"Yes."

"And all he has to do is take care of it?"

"Correct."

"But family backing gave you a chance to go adventuring? A chance to build big on your own account, like your ancestors built?"

"Exactly. Ann had the same feeling. If she were left alone, she might wish to carry on as we both planned. And I think she would need help. Need someone she could trust deeply."

"I understand." Hardisty fell back on the brutal bluntness again. "You seem certain that you'll not be at the Vuelta any more."

"Who knows? This morning we were chained. Who would have guessed that tonight we would be riding free? I am trying to plan ahead. If Ann needs you, I want you to understand everything."

"My hand on it." That was an excuse to rein in closer and reach over to Carruthers's hand. In these cool hours before dawn, the dry hot feel of the hand cried warning. The white manta cloth shirt showed no additional bleeding around the bullet hole, but what was happening deep inside? How fast was strength fading?

They were skirting a mass of tornillo scrub. The first foothills were ahead, rolling higher into these eastern offshoot mountains of the great Sierra Madre far back in the West. In the mountains ahead, Hardisty had found bonanza silver more or less by accident. Mining had been a large part of his background. His father and three roistering uncles had owned a succession of mines in Colorado, Arizona and New Mexico Territory. And ranches, also, at various times. They had been swappers, traders, developers of mines and ranches. Some years had been hugely prosperous. Other years had been belt-tightening lean.

What Hardisty remembered vividly was the constant change, even in the years he had been sent East to school. Home, through the years, had been a shifting, ever-changing background. He could remember one home: a weather-stained tent. Another home had been a Denver mansion filled with imported furniture and servants to stumble over. The next home had been a two-room adobe shack in the Black Range of New Mexico. The Denver mansion had been sold to pay for development costs of a new group of mining claims, where claim jumpers, gun battles, and ore pinching out had swallowed the Denver house money and much more.

His life had been without roots, full of change, often full of excitement. He had been educated. He knew eastern scenes, western mines, ranching and business. He could ride, shoot, fight. He knew a thousand faces, East and West, and all of it had been — and was — on the surface. There had never been time enough in one location to make close and enduring friendships.

He had thought the bonanza silver in these mountains ahead might bring his own mansion and clutter of servants. Instead, it had brought the water wheels of Don Alfredo Delgado. It had brought brutal labor and slashing whips. And all of that had toughened him as never before, and brought him close in understanding to the wild

113

Irishman, O'Meara, and this quieter Englishman, Carruthers.

The fabulous silver lode he'd found, and hidden again, would probably never be opened, Hardisty knew now. It was too deeply in Mexico. The Delgados would always be too close. But he had wandered the mountains ahead with saddle horse and pack horse. He knew the deep barrancas and high upland valleys, the springs, isolated waterholes, and faint game trails. The silver ore would not buy them life this night, or during the long, dangerous days ahead. But the rock-toughness of the water wheels and knowledge of the mountains might get them through. All of them. Even Carruthers.

Hardisty spoke quietly to the man.

"Drink all the water you want. There's more ahead. Don't punish yourself. We'll stop if you need it."

"I'll tell you."

But he wouldn't. Hardisty sensed it. Even the words sounded as if Carruthers's teeth were clenching over inner agony he would not admit.

Hardisty quested the night with eyes and ears as he heeled the Indian pony into a slow trot after the others ahead. The fighting back at the hacienda should have ended by now. There had been no higher-leaping columns of fire far back on the horizon. That could only mean the big house and fort-like barracks of the Yellow Hairs remained safe and untaken. Juan Tomás would break off and start his men for the border with what loot they had.

Rosa Lopez had draped her blanket around her shoulders, Indian-style. She had smoothed back the tangled mass of black hair and tucked it under the blanket edge. Her sleeker profile looked very young again above the shapeless blanket. She was eating something. When

Hardisty drew even with her, he saw a strip of dark jerky in her hand. She was riding easily. Her quick smile in the moonlight had warmth.

In Spanish, Hardisty said, "By tomorrow I think all the Indians will be ahead of us. It will be safe for you to ride back to the hacienda."

"You will send me away?"

"The hacienda is your home. Your people . . . ?"

She broke in, ". . . they are all dead. My *Tia* Marie, my aunt, has not wanted me. And tonight *Tia* Maria, the fat and mean one, is with the good God to whom she has prayed . . . or" — under her breath — "with the devil who deserves her."

"Rosa!"

"*¿Señor Gringo?*"

"You are a child. The hacienda is where you live. You will have to ride back as soon as it is safe. I can see you ride well. You will have no trouble."

"*¿Señor Gringo?*"

"Yes?"

"I am a woman . . . your woman, now . . . and I do not go back to that place of tears. There . . . there are bad men there. They want me like . . . like you do not want me. Beat me, *Señor Gringo*, but I will not go."

"I don't beat women."

"*¡Aie!* All men do! But I kiss your hand that holds the whip. Did you not kill for me?"

Just ahead of them, Ann Carruthers wheeled her pony back. Her words in English dripped sarcasm. "*¿Señor Gringo?* Can you get your mind off whipping women and hand-kissing long enough to suggest your plans? Mr. O'Meara doesn't seem to know. My brother doesn't. Do you?"

Subtly, her obvious dislike put him in the wrong. In the past his quick temper would have flared back. But the iron discipline of the water wheels which had kept him alive held him calm now.

"The horse herd we saw driven off through the vineyard was heading for these mountains. The rest of the Indians will follow. I'm trying to keep away from the broad plain trails they'll leave."

"Why?"

"Some of those Comanches will be in a fury against anyone not an Indian. They aren't all like Juan Tomás. They don't have any feeling about us, except for our scalps, horses, and women. They'll be dangerous. Am I plain enough?"

"Yes."

"They'll be traveling fast. I'm not sure that we could keep up, even if we wanted to. And if we're behind them, on the plain trail they'll leave, and the hacienda guards are following them, the guards will find us. Do you understand that, Miss Carruthers?"

"You make it clear enough."

Hardisty continued coolly, "We're south of the way I think the Indians will take heading for the Rio Grande. I'm hoping our trail will be lost, or at least not noticed. And I wish we could have saved old Zeke Winn, who was with you. That old man knows every trick of trailing, and knows Indians and their ways better than I ever will."

"Poor old man," Ann said sadly. "Killed because he wanted to help me."

"You didn't see his body."

"No."

"A man like Zeke Winn is never dead until you find him dead. This isn't the first Indian raid Zeke Winn has known. If he had any warning, he might have found a

116

hole to duck into."

"If I could think so. . . ."

"Try it until you hear different. Meanwhile, we're going to find a hole in those mountains ahead and stay in it until it seems safe to make for the Rio Grande. Do you have a better idea, ma'am?"

Subdued, Ann admitted, "Of course not. I haven't the slightest idea where we are or where to go. Thank you for telling me what to expect."

Chapter Eleven

When first dawn touched the eastern sky, they were climbing out of the narrow belt of foothills. As stars paled and vision reached out, not much could be seen of the higher slopes ahead. They were too steep and the scattered mesquite and cacti of the rolling grasslands was giving way to mountain brush and the first low trees.

The immense fortune in bonanza silver lay a scant day's ride from here. They would not see it or ride close to the carefully hidden outcrop. But higher, harder to find, almost inaccessible, was the hideaway Hardisty had in mind. He had discovered the place by accident. Now it could save their lives. It might save Geoffrey Carruthers's life, if the young Englishman could keep traveling through the first part of this new day.

Full dawn bloomed. The rising sun stained crimson-gold over a fleece of thin clouds hanging above the mountains. Then the full sun blaze cleared the crests. The brilliant light of the new day reached over the lower lands to the west.

Hardisty looked long and intently at the open country behind and below them. O'Meara sided him, peering back into the distance, also. Sitting hipshot, relaxed on the drooping buffalo pony, Hardisty indicated a drift of dust far to the north, nearing the mountains. "Indians? Driving horses?"

118

"Might be them Yellow Hairs," O'Meara said. He was wearing a frayed old wide-brimmed straw sombrero he had picked up in the guards' quarters back at the water wheels. The hat was cocked toward O'Meara's left eye and, with the dark, heavy beard stubble on the square face, gave him a raffish, villainous look.

Hardisty grinned faintly at the Irishman. They had suffered together. Until Carruthers was brought to the water wheels, the only hope, comfort and companionship in the savage little world where they had been chained had been each other.

"Not Yellow Hairs," Hardisty differed. "To get where that dust is now, they'd have had to start hours ago, in the middle of the night. D'you think they'd move out into the open until full daylight?"

O'Meara grinned back. They could argue and differ, sometimes heatedly, scornfully, but a kind of unspoken, deep affection was now a lifelong bond between them. It colored all their contacts with each other. O'Meara's shrug agreed.

"And you can bet," Hardisty added, "that Juan Tomás took every horse and mule his men could find. It'll take hours, or a full day, to bring in more horses."

Rosa Lopez was still wrapped in the old blanket that had also come out of the guards' quarters. Scuffed leather sandals were on her feet. In the morning light, her skin was soft olive, her nose straight, mouth full, black lashes long over brown, curious eyes that were regarding Hardisty with grave approval. Her smile flashed at him, friendly and provocative.

"*Señor Gringo*, I am good cook. I will make little fire and cook for you, no?"

"We will not have fire here, Rosa." They were speaking in Spanish, the only language she knew. "We will eat pinole." Hardisty looked at the gaunt, strained face of Geoffrey Carruthers and dismounted. "Rest here," he said to all.

Ann, who understood Spanish, spoke in English after she slipped off her horse, while Rosa Lopez watched her in close, enigmatic interest. "I have never eaten pinole."

Hardisty chuckled dryly. "It's not fried chicken. Merely parched corn ground fine, with sugar added, and then water before it's eaten. A quick meal in a tin cup. You can travel far and fast on a little pinole. We were lucky to find a bag of it."

"You . . . you were fed that at the water wheels? Corn meal and water?"

"Some meals. It always tasted good."

Carruthers had slid awkwardly from his horse. He staggered, and steadied himself by gripping the pony's mane. In the new sunlight, perspiration glinted on his forehead. Hardisty made no comment as the Englishman dropped down against an outcrop of yellow sandstone and went passively limp, closing his eyes.

Ann dropped to a knee beside him. "Jeff, dear! Are you this weak?"

The eyes opened. Carruthers smiled, the corners of his mouth paling with the effort, but he smiled. "Is it against rules to be tired after a long ride?"

Her hand touched his cheek. "You're feverish."

"Thirsty, I suppose. Emptied m'canteen two hours ago."

One of the small water *ollas* was slung across Hardisty's shoulder. He spoke gruffly as he reached down for the empty canteen.

"Why the devil didn't you say so? I told you there was water ahead, and to drink all you wanted." He emptied the *olla* into the canteen, and told Ann briefly, "Fix him pinole in your tin cup. Rosa or O'Meara will show you how."

"Please don't take your temper out on a wounded, sick man!" Her cheeks were hot, her eyes hated him as she turned to the food sack across her pony's withers.

Hardisty ignored her.

"Carruthers, you know you need water as well as food. Take care of yourself."

"Sorry. Foolish, wasn't it? I was thirsty, and I wasn't thirsty. I'll get Ann straightened out."

"Half a day's more riding. Mostly up. If you can't make it, say so. There's water this side of where I want to get. We'll stop."

Rosa Lopez came to Hardisty's elbow, her forefinger giving a last stir to the contents of her tin cup. "*Señor Gringo,* your pinole."

Hardisty handed the cup to Carruthers.

"Drink it, then try to chew some jerky. Or a hunk of that goat cheese we brought. It's rank, but good for you."

Serious as the man's condition was, Geoffrey Carruthers remained the gentleman. He lifted the cup of pinole slightly, forcing another pale-cornered smile past Hardisty's arm at Rosa Lopez.

"*Gracias, señorita.*"

Chapter Twelve

This was the morning when Don Alfredo Correon de Leon y Delgado gazed upon the reeking shambles that the night had left. Smoke still lifted from the fire-gutted *jacales*, huts, outbuildings. Black-and-gray ash heaps lay where the huge haystacks had been. The vineyard, pride of the hacienda, had been ripped and trampled by surging horses.

The scalped dead, young and old, were scattered throughout the charred wreckage, but none of the dead — thanks to the good God — were of the blood of de Leon y Delgado. Many commissary accounts would now go unpaid. Strong and docile peons would have to be replaced. There would be the usual shortage of women and children after an Indian raid. And in this hour of sunrise not a horse or a mule was in sight. But none of that really mattered. There were more horses. New haystacks would rise. *Jacales* would be rebuilt. Too many ignorant peons infested the country as it was. A man could shrug off such losses as the will of God.

What did matter to Don Alfredo Delgado this sunrise hour was his cut, torn, bruised and bandaged head. Hatred that he had not thought possible — hatred that would live always with him now — seeped through his veins like acid. In front of his wife and daughter-in-law, he had been whipped with a chain. He, Don Alfredo Delgado, most macho of men, whose pride and courage were notorious, had cringed before his women like a beaten *pelado,* and had run across the patio with the chain whipping his back, and his bowels knotted with fear of more pain.

When he thought of the big, young *yanqui* who had brought in the bonanza silver ore and then defied him, who had slashed him with the chain in cold, callous fury last night, a silent scream of hatred geysered inside his bandaged head. To the death, that *yanqui!*

Capitán Sanchez, in charge of the hacienda guards, reported at the front gate.

"The devils are gone, *patrón.* It is not yet possible to count the dead, or the missing women and children."

"It was Comanches?"

"*Si, patrón.* Comanches."

"You have told the men . . . fifty pesos for each Indian head brought here to the gate?"

"*Si, patrón,* they are collecting a few heads now."

"And the three *gringo* men?"

Capitán Sanchez was a stocky man, wide-shouldered, bowlegged from a lifetime in the saddle. Gray hairs speckled his formidable black mustache. The cartridge belts crossed over the yellow vest of hair spotted calfskin, the two revolvers, the carbine in one hand and the high-crowned, wide-brimmed straw hat in the other hand, marked him a hard, efficient man.

Sanchez was all of that, a man bred, born, raised on the hacienda. He had been young when Don Alfredo was young. There was understanding between them, and in this sunrise hour there was also chill fear trickling through Sanchez when the three *gringos* were thrown between his teeth. Last night in the heat of fighting off Comanches, he had seen Don Alfredo's torn and bleeding face. Briefly

123

he had been within earshot of the vitriolic, near-hysterical threats if the *yanquis* came through this night alive and were brought again in chains. Sanchez had lifelong knowledge and gut-twisting fear of how dangerous Don Alfredo's rages could be.

He replied now, uneasily, "The men, *patrón,* are looking. They have not found *yanqui* bodies. Only the irons, *patrón.* The leg irons and the wrist irons."

"Fool! Offal! Vomit of a pig! You stand there knowing this and say nothing!"

"In the vineyard, *patrón.* All the irons together and tracks of Indian horses leading from that spot to the water wheels."

"Imbecile! *¡Chongo! ¡Cabrón!* You should be chained on the wheels! Why should they ride back to the wheels?"

"For the food, *patrón.* They took all the food. The blankets, the water *ollas,* tin cups. All. And rode away. Angelo Roybal, my best tracker, swears it is so. They left early in the night riding east. The sign was cold."

"East?"

"*Si.*"

"Where the Comanches will ride."

"*Si.*"

"These are *gringos!*"

"*Si,* but they ride toward Texas, *patrón.* Are we to turn our back on what God has given us? The trail they left is plain. Five horses . . . east."

"Ox of the devil! Pay attention!"

"*Patrón.* . . ."

"Thou hast known me, boy and man."

"*Si, patrón,* boy and man."

"Thou hast judgment of what I promise. I will have the skin in little strips from any man who turns back from these cursed *yanquis!*"

"You wish the Comanches, also, *patrón?*"

"God's suffering blood! The Comanches will be halfway to Texas before there are horses to follow that many. I care nothing now for the cursed Comanches. They came to my father and my grandfather, and they will come to my sons. But for the head of the *gringo* Irishman: here on the ground at this gate, I will pay five thousand pesos. For the Englishman's head: five thousand pesos. And for the head of that big *gringo* who brought in the silver ore, ten thousand pesos here at the gate when his head rolls out of the sack!"

"Holy saints, *patrón!* They will be friends of the devil on the trail. Wait with confidence, *patrón.*"

"I will wait, Sanchez. For years, if necessary. . . ."

Chapter Thirteen

The steep wash was a pale gash in the flank of the mountain. It writhed and twisted, undercutting masses of rock, its bed littered with huge boulders and smaller rocks. Finer gravels and sand had been scoured far down the mountain by infrequent torrents of storm water.

At midmorning, with the sun blazing in a cloudless sky, the wash was an oven of baking rock. O'Meara was leading. Hardisty was riding last, where he could watch Geoffrey Carruthers, just ahead of him. The Englishman was riding with head and shoulders deeply bowed. Occasionally he clutched at his pony's tangled mane and held on. Without water, the man would have been on the ground by now, helpless, Hardisty guessed. And Carruthers might slide limply off at any minute.

Ahead of O'Meara the wash narrowed, sides almost vertical. An eight foot wall of rock blocked further advance up the wash.

"Left, up into the brush and trees," Hardisty called. The buffalo ponies were as nimble as goats. Putting his mount to the climb, Hardisty now took the lead. O'Meara, without being ordered, dropped back to the rear, where he could watch Carruthers.

Half an hour later Hardisty was guiding them around big rock outthrusts, on slanting footing of rotten shale. Bits of dislodged rock rattled down the steep slope and leaped into space not twenty yards away. The drop-off plunged into a deep, narrow barranca filled with blue, smoky shadows.

Hardisty called back, "Let the horses do it all. They won't slip!"

When the rotten shale ledges were behind, Ann Carruthers spoke with edged animosity. "How much more of this must my brother endure?"

"About an hour. He'll make it."

"And if he can't . . . ?"

"We'll stop. But I'm heading to a seep spring with good water. We can have a small, smokeless fire, and be comfortable and safe."

What he didn't mention was a nagging worry of the past several hours, after he had thought of the wrist and leg irons hastily discarded in the vineyard. At the time, with the Comanche attack filling the night, the shackles had not seemed to matter. But now it was obvious that those shackles pin-pointed their start. Any good tracker could follow their sign from the vineyard to the water wheels, and then east, apart from the trails the Comanches would be leaving. Every shackle and length of chain should have been gathered up and hurled, say, into the bottom mud under the water wheels. Then their sign would have seemed more like Indian sign.

Hardisty could have groaned. The shackles were markers, pointing after them. And it was a waste of emotion to wonder if Don Alfredo Delgado would want them followed. He would.

They crossed high benches where the horses dipped heads and snatched mouthfuls of bunch grass. They followed another wash steeply up, and came out on a still higher bench where rock walls on two sides went up straight a full hundred feet. Seep water crept out of a fissure in one of the rock walls and slid down into a small rock depression, and from there overflowed across the bench in a green swath, and sank back into the earth.

"We'll camp here," Hardisty said. He helped Geoffrey Carruthers off the horse, and made no comment about the man's slack weight and leaden movements. It was as if Carruthers had used the last of his strength, and forced himself past the breaking point by sheer power of will. "I found this place by accident," Hardisty told them. "Over there are the ashes of my old fire. No one else seems to have camped here since."

They had brought coffee and a soot-blackened coffee pot. While Hardisty was starting a fire, a small fire, Ann Carruthers spread her blanket and coaxed her brother flat on it. His eyes closed again.

She came to Hardisty, speaking under her breath, desperately, "There must be something you can do for him."

"His trouble is inside, ma'am. I don't know how bad it is. Anything I'd try might make it worse than it is now. Letting him rest is the best thing we can do for him. . . . O'Meara and I are going to be busy. You ladies will have to cook."

"We will," Ann said absently. Her mind was still on her brother.

A hawk skimmed close overhead. A bluejay gave raucous protest at these strange intruders. O'Meara had taken the single reins of the horses and was watering the animals.

"How long you aim to stay here?" O'Meara asked when Hardisty joined him.

"There's good grass and another seep spring in a mountain meadow about a quarter of a mile back through those trees. I stopped here so we wouldn't be surprised by anyone trailing us. In that open meadow, we could be surrounded and not know it."

"You didn't think there was much chance we'd be followed."

"Changed my mind. We left those wrist and leg irons in the vineyard. Our trail started there. If Delgado wants us bad enough, we can be followed."

O'Meara gave a low, rueful whistle.

"Carruthers," O'Meara said flatly, "can't go on. Not for days . . . if he's here that long."

"He can rest now. Both the girls need rest and sleep, also."

O'Meara yawned and grinned. "They ain't the only ones. It's been a night!"

They were talking quietly while the horses drank.

"If I'm right," said Hardisty thoughtfully, "anyone following us will have to stay on our trail exactly. They won't know we're here. We have three revolvers. I'll take two of them and backtrack on foot. You take the horses to that meadow grass. About mid-afternoon I'll meet you here, and you can go back down our trail and watch. Don't lose a horse. This is no place for any of us to be afoot."

"If them damn Yellow Hairs come along with their carbines, you won't stand a chance with revolvers. All they got to do is stay off a little ways and shoot the hell outa' your liver an' lights."

"If trouble starts, I'll be in close where a hand-gun stands a chance. Anyway, it can't happen for hours. I'll catch some sleep and backtrack. If you hear shooting, have the horses ready to ride. Don't try running to help me."

"Faith now, am I that foolish? The divil himself will be tellin' me to ride off with the girls and keep healthy. It fair brings tears when I think how easy the divil wins out on me."

O'Meara was grinning, promising nothing. Two hours later, with food in his stomach, and a brief, sodden sleep, Hardisty was backtracking their trail. He went a full half-mile before finding what he wanted.

A wash here cut deeply into the mountain. The slanted sides were steep and littered with huge rocks. But the narrow bed of the wash itself held no rocks large enough to shelter a man. Hardisty picked a spot close in, where lichen-spotted boulders gave shelter from almost any angle.

He could see down the bone-dry channel for better than a hundred yards. Upstream the scoured, baking channel climbed steeply over rock ledges. At this point they had dismounted, all but Carruthers, and led their horses over those ledges.

The mountain air high above the lowlands had a new crispness, but the midday strike of the sun put broiling heat into the rocks, the dry earth, and the air between them. There was no cooling breeze. The silence was profound.

Hardisty had brought a water *olla,* one gun-belt and two revolvers, both .44 caliber. He carefully checked the guns once more, slid one back into the belt holster, and the other inside the cracked leather belt of his ripped, filthy pants. He looked down at the pants. His smile went wry as he touched the heavy stubble on his face, felt his long uncut hair, and had some idea of how he must look to the two girls. A wild, villainous, undoubtedly desperate stranger. But not — and it was not too unpleasant to think about now — but not all that to Rosa Lopez. His woman . . . for the asking, . . . the taking.

The heat and silence were making him drowsy again. A squirrel came across the ground with small, silent rushes, saw him there among the rocks and streaked off, vanishing. Here in the quiet peace of the mountain, all else seemed far away, unreal. Last night might not have happened. When one thought about it drowsily, this cautious vigil on their backtrail did seem foolish.

Hardisty shook off the feeling, gulped cool water from the *olla*, and forced himself into keen alertness. The great, ponderous water wheels on the Delgado hacienda had been real enough. The wild, gruesome details of the Comanche raid had not been dreamed. And when Hardisty put the cold clarity of memory on Don Alfredo Delgado, no aspect of the man suggested peace or safety. Not that bleeding wreck of a face which had been his last view of Delgado.

Still nothing happened. Hours crawled into early afternoon. The heat shimmering off the naked rocks grew worse. What did not happen today, might happen tomorrow. The danger existed. Only foolish recklessness would ignore it. And if it did happen, what could one man and two short-range revolvers do about it?

The drowsiness was pressing in again when Hardisty heard jaybirds in excited racket somewhere beyond the first descending bend in the wash. He was instantly alert. Some danger was moving down there, exciting the jays. But when the first rider appeared, and a second rider, and a third, it had again, an unreal quality. Yellow Hairs, close, dangerous. . . .

Each man wore the spotted yellow calfskin vest with hair outside, and crossed cartridge belts and wide-brimmed straw sombrero. They were riding in a single file, the point man following without difficulty the tracks of five horses which had come up the bed of the wash this midmorning. A fourth man rode into sight . . . a fifth man . . . a sixth.

131

Taut now, Hardisty cocked the gun that had been shoved inside his pants belt. He wondered how long he could hold out against a dozen or two of these Yellow Hairs. Not long. Too many men, too many guns which they well knew how to use. Once more everything arrogant and evil about the Delgados seemed to be reaching out for victims. Six of them in sight now.

The seventh man did not appear. Six seemed to be all, for the time being at least. Hardisty drew a slow breath. Now he had a chance. The Yellow Hairs were riding with loose ease, which suggested they'd often trailed like this, and had no doubt of the outcome. And still the seventh man did not appear.

Number Four man called in Spanish, "Are they going to the top of the cursed mountain?"

Number One man turned in the saddle. "I think a little camp somewhere high up. They are not Comanches, only *gringos,* tired and hungry, who think they are not followed."

Number Two man sounded reverent. "Twenty thousand pesos for three heads in a sack. My grandfather would not believe this."

Number Three said, "Pah! I do not believe either, until I see Don Alfredo's pesos in my hand and feel the mescal burning my gullet."

Number Five said, "Mescal? *¡Aie!* What is mescal but a headache? I will take the young woman. The sweet-smelling young *gringo* woman who will know a man, finally. A real man!"

"The woman to you, and welcome, *compadre.* I have too many women now. You can have this *gringo* woman, this *gringa,* while the line waits. Me . . . I only want the ten thousand peso head."

This was real! Three heads in a sack. Twenty thousand

pesos. One head worth ten thousand pesos. And Ann Carruthers for all of them.

Hardisty could guess whose head in a sack was worth ten thousand pesos. His head, of course — he who had lashed rusty manacle chains across Delgado's face. Ten thousand pesos for Hardisty's head in a sack was a measure of the Don's implacable hatred. But it was the thought of Ann Carruthers's being given to these men that filled Hardisty with chill, calculating anger.

He stayed down out of sight until the first click and strike of metal-shod hoofs was past. Until the second man rode past. Quite calmly then, Hardisty raised up, rested the revolver barrel across his crooked left arm, sighted carefully, and drove the third man reeling out of his saddle.

Five riders left and, as he had planned, the orderly advance was suddenly in wild confusion. While the first two men were frantically wheeling their horses in the narrow bed of the wash, Hardisty with cold care sighted on the fourth man and knocked him reeling in the saddle, then falling with a second shot.

Four left now, separated by the two horses of dead or dying men. Hardisty was fast because he had to be fast. He was deliberate because wasted shots could mean the difference between life and death. They knew where he was now. Their guns were out and the first wild shots were seeking him.

Chapter Fourteen

Number Two man was nearest. He was jerking his carbine out of the boot as he savagely wheeled the roan horse back. Knotted reins dropped over the horn of the heavy Mexican saddle as the carbine muzzle came up. Hardisty sighted the revolver again and squeezed the trigger and, suddenly, the nose on the dark, mustached face became a gory hole.

Bad shooting. That one had been aimed for the high chest. But he was above the riders, shooting down at them, and the targets were moving fast. The man's head was driven back by the bullet shock. The wheeling horse lunged to the right, then halted, and the rider slid far over and kept going out of the saddle.

A bullet struck rock near Hardisty's leg and screamed off at an angle. A second bullet brushed his left arm high up, leaving holes in the shirt sleeve and starting blood. That would be Number Five who was frantically levering his carbine. That was the man who had bid for Ann Carruthers instead of mescal. Hardisty's answering shot missed. His second shot struck the man's horse and his gun was empty. He shoved it inside his pants belt and had the holstered revolver out a second later.

The plunging Number Five horse, blood streaming from a bullet gash in his neck, was making the rider an uncertain target. And the man could not set himself to try accurately with his carbine.

Two, then three gunshots up the wash drew Hardisty's fast look at Number One rider. The man had dropped his carbine and was bent over the saddle horn, hands clutching the horse's mane. The wide-brimmed straw hat with rawhide *barboquejo* strings hanging loose was sliding off as the man bowed far over, trying desperately to stay in the saddle.

A deep-lunged yell of satisfaction not much different from a Comanche war whoop drew Hardisty's gaze to the rock ledges up the wash. O'Meara was on one of the lower ledges, grinning like a satisfied fury as he emptied his revolver at the riders in the wash.

Two left out of six, one of them on a wounded horse. O'Meara's sudden appearance finished unnerving them. Spinning their horses, gouging big-roweled Mexican spurs, the two fled back the way they had come. Hardisty emptied his revolver after them and thought he hit Number Five — but the man stayed in the saddle and vanished around the bend in the wash.

Revolver in hand, Hardisty was already descending the steep bank. Four riderless horses were milling uncertainly, two of them ground-tied by dragging reins. Two men were dead. Two were still breathing as O'Meara grabbed the reins of the other two horses.

Hardisty was accusing. "Told you not to come if shooting started."

"I didn't," O'Meara said, unabashed. "I was hid up there, waiting."

"I didn't hear you come."

"I'm sneaky."

"What about the horses you were supposed to be watching?"

"That girl, that Rosa, your woman, is watchin' 'em,"

said O'Meara innocently. "You might say it was her doing. Would I let her man get killed while I hung around camp watchin' women and horses? She shamed me, laddie, so I wrestled with the divil an' lost, and then tested how close a man could sneak up on you."

"Too close." Hardisty was rueful. "And I needed you after all. Man! Look at what we've got. Carbines, canteens, revolvers, cartridges, knives, saddlebags stuffed with food, hobbles, ropes, saddles, blankets, horses. . . ."

"And two men riding back for help," O'Meara reminded.

"Ask that man you helped knock off his horse. He was leading. His eyes are closed but he's faking. Ask him how much help is coming and how far away it is."

O'Meara bent over the man and spoke in Spanish.

"This is one of the guards who jumped me when I punched young Delgado. I think he's the one hit me from behind with his gun barrel. Another bullet in him might make his eyes open."

"Try it," Hardisty said in Spanish. "We don't have time to waste."

The eyes opened. "*¡Señor!* By the Virgin and Her mercy. . . ."

"How many more men coming after us?" O'Meara demanded.

"How can I say, *Señor?* We were the first. They were bringing in more horses."

"More coming after us?"

"*Sí.* Many. It is the will of the *patrón.* Mercy, *Señor.* . . ."

"Ain't a one of 'em ever heard of mercy until a knife was at their throats or a gun muzzle in their teeth," O'Meara said disgustedly.

Hardisty was taking gun-belts and guns off the dead

men. "Keep him talking. Everything he knows. Might be a gaggle of them only a couple of miles away."

Minutes later, O'Meara said, "That's all he seems to know. Plenty more coming after us when they get horses to ride." O'Meara spat disgustedly. "Ten thousand pesos for your head in a sack. But me . . . I'm only worth five thousand! Ain't that a howdy-do?"

Hardisty chuckled. Carbines had been returned to saddle boots. Shell belts and revolvers were hung over saddle horns. Canteens were in place. Knives had been removed from the dead men and the living. But moments later O'Meara's uncertain astonishment blurted, "You undressin' them dead men?"

"Yes," Hardisty said, unruffled. "The girls need pants and shirts for what's ahead. This is the only place to get them."

O'Meara whistled. "This is one store they'll never go shopping in alone. You leavin' these two wounded men here in the wash?"

"Can't take 'em along. Can't help them, except to leave a canteen of water. More men from the hacienda will be along and find them. Got a better idea?"

"Nope."

"Then get the clothes off that other dead one. We can't even guess how much time we have and, when they come again, there'll be more than six!"

Ann Carruthers spoke with cold finality. "I will not dress like a man and certainly not in clothes stripped from a dead man!"

She was standing by the blanket where her brother lay. The small cookfire had dwindled to lazy-smoking embers. Geoffrey Carruthers seemed a bit stronger. His voice was steady.

"Ann, you aren't exactly at your best, riding astride

with long skirts."

The color in her cheeks was visible. "What else can I do?"

"Stop talking like an idiot whose virtue depends on the length of her skirt."

Hardisty watched silently, pants, shirt and yellow calf-skin vest over his left arm. Only a brother could talk like that and not be cut off by her scorn.

Rosa Lopez called in Spanish, "How I look, *Señor Gringo?*"

Without argument she had vanished among the nearest trees with the clothes Hardisty had handed her. In brief minutes she had changed. The dead man had been short and wiry. Pants, shirt and vest fitted her snugly. A little too snugly in the shirt, for now there was no doubt that Rosa Lopez was a mature young girl.

"Like a pretty boy, Rosa."

"Hah! Not boy! I am woman. Much woman. Your woman, *Señor Gringo.*" She caught up one of the wide-brimmed, high-crowned sombreros which O'Meara had brought in and dropped on the ground. With the hat jauntily on her head and the *barboquejo* strings dangling beside her olive cheeks, Rosa said, "Look! I am very fierce Yellow Hair woman, no?"

O'Meara was grinning again. "If all them Yellow Hairs was like this, why, faith, I'd wait all day for them."

Geoffrey Carruthers said, "Ann, this isn't England or the ranch. The man is dead. It won't matter to him."

Ann was looking thoughtfully at Rosa Lopez. Silently, she took the clothes off Hardisty's arm, picked up one of the sombreros, and walked toward the trees.

Rosa Lopez giggled.

"I know she will do it when she sees me. She is much woman, too," Rosa said in her rippling Spanish. "So I

138

let her see how a man looks at me like this. *¡Aie!* You think she will go on riding like a silly old woman with her skirts hunched up when the men are looking at me, so?"

O'Meara's shout of laughter followed. He used Spanish, too. "Jesus and Mary! A little Mexican *bruja* who knows all the answers." Even Carruthers forced a brief, strained smile.

Hardisty had waved the Mexican girl away when she had noticed blood on his left sleeve. The shallow bullet gash had stopped bleeding and would be all right.

Carruthers was the problem. Neither O'Meara nor Hardisty had mentioned the thousands of pesos of reward money for their heads. They would not. Hardisty was matter-of-fact now as he spoke to the young Englishman.

"One of these saddles should make riding easier for you."

"I take it," Carruthers said calmly, "that our only chance now is to ride day and night and keep ahead of them."

How could you tell a gallant young man who showed no fear that he must ride until he died, or stay behind and be murdered? You could look at him and accept the fact that his head cut off and carried back to the hacienda in a sack was worth five thousand pesos. But you couldn't tell him, even though you knew it was probably going to happen. How right was a man in deciding that from now on there would be no more waiting and resting until they were all captured?

"East of here," Hardisty told the young Englishman, "is a high mountain valley which will take us north. We should cut the Comanche trail that way. Each of you will have a saddle now. I'll ride my Indian pony. We'll take the others on lead ropes. No matter how bright the moon is these nights, we'll leave a trail that will take daylight to follow. But we can be traveling all day and part of the night, and so keep ahead."

"If the girls can stand it."

"They'll have to." Hardisty said it with cool finality.

Carruthers showed no awareness that this talk was really about himself. Could he stand the punishing pace? And if not, then what? He was calmer than Hardisty when he said, "I don't think anyone will hold the others back."

O'Meara's admiring whistle drew their glances. Ann was returning. She had rolled up the pants slightly at the bottoms. But in pants, shirt, and vest she was straight-shouldered and slim-waisted. Her thick brown hair with glints of gold had been tucked up under the wide-brimmed straw sombrero. The New Mexico sun had dusted her smooth skin with golden tan. She was composed, but her eyes held a smoky, challenging look.

"*¡Aie!*" Rosa Lopez said critically in Spanish. "Maybe it is better you don't dress like this around my *gringo*. I think he don't look at me so much now."

In her schoolbook Spanish, Ann said, "Your *gringo* is yours as much as he wants."

"Hah! I make him want."

O'Meara was grinning again. Hardisty ignored all of it. "We're moving out as fast as possible. Canteens and *ollas* have to be filled. Saddles reset. You girls will have shell belts, revolvers, and carbines. Both of you will stay close to me. O'Meara will ride well back, where he can watch the back-trail. Any questions?"

No questions, but there was a sadness and strain in Ann Carruthers's eyes when she looked at the pallid face of her brother.

Each of the girls was now astride a saddled horse and had the lead rope of an Indian pony. O'Meara, his protests overridden by Hardisty, had a saddled horse and the lead ropes of the other two ponies. Carruthers was riding more comfortably in a deep Mexican saddle with stirrups, and no lead rope to make demands on his failing strength.

Hardisty, still on his buffalo pony, had no lead rope either and carried the carbine from the boot of Rosa Lopez's saddle. All the rest of the long afternoon he forced the pace, knowing what it was doing to Carruthers, and knowing it had to be done. Pursuit might be just out of sight behind them. Useless to try to hide their trail by scattering. Neither Carruthers nor the girls could safely ride off alone. They had to be guided by Hardisty.

The high, narrow, north-reaching valley they followed was a rough trough between rougher ridges and rock escarpments. Stretches of mountain grass alternated between tangles of scrub oak and pine and undergrowth. The dry sands of a shallow little arroyo reached north with them. Then, fed by seep springs, the sands were damp. Finally a narrow run of water moved lazily north.

Hardisty let the horses drink sparingly. The afternoon was running out fast. Night would hide their tracks, but it would also hide the Indian trail to the Rio Grande. Buzzards found it for them. An obscure umbrella of dark wings ahead was circling lower and lower.

"Comanches passed there," Hardisty guessed.

Carruthers asked in strained huskiness, "Will the girls be safe?"

"As safe as they'll be if the hacienda guards catch us."

"In other words, probably not . . . ?"

"The risk has to be taken."

"I've told Ann what to do with her revolver if she's helpless with those guards or the Indians."

Hardisty nodded. He had abrasive thoughts about what probably would happen when a girl was faced with putting

141

a bullet into her own head or submitting to multiple rape.

Had there been no buzzards, the Indian trail still would have been easy to recognize. The earth was trampled over a sizable area by the passing of hundreds of hoofs. The shallow banks of the arroyo were cut and torn by the horses that had crowded down to the water.

Off to one side as O'Meara rode to investigate, a clot of buzzards lifted into flight with clumsy flapping of broad wings.

O'Meara's lurid oath was followed by his harsh warning, "Don't let them ladies come here!"

Ann Carruthers made the decision.

"We had better know. We are facing the same thing." In Spanish she said, "Rosa, come."

It was a young woman. Her skirts had been pulled up over her head in an orgy of lust and gratification and, afterwards, she had been lanced to death.

Rosa Lopez looked and gulped, "Guadalupe Chavez! She was to . . . to marry. . . ." The slender, boy-like figure wheeled her horse away from the sight, retching, crying unashamededly.

Ann's pallor was intense as she accused Hardisty.

"These are the savages you are trying to join?"

"Not the ones who did this. I'm trying to find Chief Juan Tomás and his son. I think they're a better gamble than what we're running from."

"For you men, perhaps. Are . . . are you going to leave her here like this?"

"Don't have a shovel. Can't take time to cover her with rocks. We're not trying to be civilized. We're running for our lives. Can you understand that?"

"I understand," she said in thin, cold bitterness. "It's, 'Everyone for himself and the devil take the others,' isn't it?"

A smaller clot of buzzards flapped away from a dead child, a small boy whose head had been crushed by the rock which had been tossed down beside the body.

Ann asked fiercely, "Why would they bring him this far and then kill him?"

"Might be he tried to run away, or was crying and making a nuisance of himself," Hardisty told her. "The 'whys' aren't important. It happened. There's nothing we can do about it."

Geoffrey Carruthers had not bothered to ride over and look at the bodies. He clutched the horn of his saddle much of the time. A gray pallor had settled on his ravaged face. When Hardisty rode to his side, the Englishman said harshly, "I can go on."

"How long?"

"How do I know? If I ask to be left here, will the rest of you ride on?"

"I don't think your sister would."

"Make her! Tie her to the saddle! For her own good!"

"I'm not ready for that."

"You'd better be getting ready, if you're going to help her with the Vuelta like you promised."

That promise seemed distant and not much more than kind words. Layer by layer, Hardisty reflected as they rode on, the best of civilization was being stripped from them. Only brutal realities mattered now.

They passed a dead mule and more buzzards, and the broad, hoof-churned trail struck up the eastern ridge toward a gap which was plainly the easiest way to get east through these mountains.

They were climbing rapidly when O'Meara called from the rear, "Here they come! Trailin' us!"

The yellow calfskin vests were visible first in the shadows creeping over the valley floor. Eight . . . twelve

. . . seventeen yellow vests strung out on spurred, running horses.

"We'll wait for them up where that pass cuts through the ridge," Hardisty decided. He looked at his companions. They were five — and seventeen tough, disciplined fighting men were trailing them down. Of the five, two were girls, one was a dying man, visibly swaying now in the saddle. Four carbines against seventeen carbines. . . .

O'Meara asked, "Any chance of keeping ahead of 'em?"

"Not now."

The Indian trail was broad and plain up into the pass where the steep side slopes were a jumble of rocks, scrub trees, and brush. Hardisty looked swiftly around.

"O'Meara, Carruthers, tie your horses over there on the north side and get down out of sight. We'll do the same on the south side."

Ann said evenly, "I'd rather be with my brother."

"I want him with O'Meara. We'll hold them off as long as possible. They could get discouraged."

"Do you think so?"

"No," Hardisty admitted.

The first twilight was spreading blue shadows on the valley floor. There was more light up here in the pass as they hastily tied horses to the scrub trees and selected rocks to use for cover.

"¿Señor Gringo?"

"Yes?"

"This is the end, no?"

"You are of the hacienda. They will take you home."

"Hah! Those cabrónes! They will take me into the bushes like Guadalupe Chavez. Señor, when it is time, you will shoot me, no? But not in the face. I do not

144

want my face shot."

Ann Carruthers, very pale now, said coolly in English, "I'll shoot myself if it has to be done. Is that clear?"

"Get your guns and cartridges ready. They'll be here in a few minutes."

O'Meara's call from the opposite slope had an odd dumbfounded sound. "Comanches are hid out all over this damn slope! And payin' us no mind!"

"Then they don't want you," Hardisty called back. "Juan Tomás must be here somewhere." To the girls he said, "Get those yellow vests off. Leave those sombreros on the ground so every Indian will know you're women and not more hacienda guards."

Hardisty stood up again, turning to scan the slope where brush and scrub growth were thick among the rocks. He called, "Juan Tomás!"

And got no answer.

Knowing Indians must be there somewhere, he still needed moments of close watching before he made out an unblinking eye at the corner of a lichen-splotched boulder. Then legs and moccasined feet behind another sizable rock. Bushes, trees, rocks were sheltering prone, waiting Comanches.

Hardisty gripped his carbine tighter when a Comanche in breech-clout, moccasins, and red, yellow and black war paint, shell belt across his torso, carbine ready in his hand, appeared from behind a tree trunk and glided silently down the slope toward him.

"Juanito!" Hard to fit this painted young Comanche warrior with the morose, shackled prisoner on the water wheels only yesterday.

"I t'ink better I stay with you."

"Where's Juan Tomás?"

Juanito gestured vaguely up the slope behind them.

145

"Las' night too much fort, like you say. They follow us, maybe to Texas. So Juan Tomás wait here in his fort." The boldly painted face smiled slightly. "One trap this, huh? An' you come an' bring them into trap." Juanito indicated Ann, using his chin, Indian-style, instead of pointing. "Your wife, huh?"

"Who? Oh, yes, my wife."

Red flushed into Ann's pale face. But she remembered last night and held silence.

"You have babies?"

"Not yet."

"You have two women."

"I took the other one last night. She speaks only Spanish."

Juanito nodded, neither surprised nor much interested. "I t'ink they come," he said, going flat on the earth beside Hardisty.

The hacienda men were bunched now. Bit chains jingling, leather creaking, shod hoofs clashing on rocks, they came into the narrow pass. Seventeen riders, confident, only slightly wary now, for the Indian sign was hours old and only five fugitives were close ahead. Seventeen hunting five — and three of the five heads worth twenty thousand pesos. Some such thoughts must have filled even Capitán Sanchez. A man could get drunk with anticipation just thinking about twenty thousand silver pesos. Could forget even caution, such as sending a man or two ahead to flush out another possible ambush. They were well into the pass before a Yellow Hair shouted and pointed toward the horses tied in the brush behind O'Meara and Carruthers.

O'Meara shot him. The flat slam of the carbine report was followed by O'Meara's great-lunged howl of derision. "Five thousand pesos! Come and get it!"

146

While the Yellow Hair was reeling in the saddle, Hardisty shot the man next to him, and then went flat to earth as a storm of gunfire on both slopes of the pass tore the first twilight shadows.

Guns — dozens of guns and high, fierce warwhoops — filled the narrow pass with slamming violence. Horses went down screaming. Saddles emptied. The hacienda guards fired instinctively and futilely at targets still all but invisible. And abruptly, not a half-minute after O'Meara's first shot, the hacienda horses wheeled back in hard-spurred retreat. Hardisty counted eleven riders now. One of the eleven was shot out of the saddle while he watched.

Juanito was laughing as he stood up. "I t'ink we go now to Texas easy."

"Hardisty!" That was O'Meara shouting.

"Yes?"

"Carruthers! He stood up an' got it this time. He wanted it this way. Told me so."

Chapter Fifteen

In Santa Fe, in his plain office just off the plaza, Simon Roddan leaned back in his desk chair and listened to his visitor with cool intentness. Jack Cultus had just made the dusty, bone-jarring stagecoach trip back from the border country. The man's dark broadcloth suit and flowered silk vest had taken on the wrinkled, grimy-dusty look of continuous wear. Even the black mustache shot with gray needed trimming.

"And that's what happened," Cultus finished.

Roddan was blunt. "It's the damndest yarn I've heard this year. You trail a man across the border. You know he started from Azul to the Delgado hacienda, but he never got there. So you went on to Chihuahua to see if he'd gone that way. But he hadn't. He'd just vanished. On the way back, you checked at Azul again, and the sister had been there and had gone out to the hacienda. And Comanches had raided the hacienda and carried her off."

The flat, hoarse voice of Jack Cultus was sourly resentful. "The hell with whether you believe it or not, that's what happened!"

Simon Roddan smiled thinly.

"I believe you, because you aren't swearing the Englishman is dead and aren't trying to collect the thousand dollar bet we had that his health would stay good. All you claim is that he vanished."

"That's right."

"And Comanches got the sister."

"They must have got her. There was a big Comanche raid. Plenty others on the hacienda were killed or taken. Why would anyone lie about this girl?"

Roddan whistled softly, tunelessly, while he thought about it. "Too bad," he finally said. "She's dead by now, I suppose, or might as well be dead."

It had been Simon Roddan's pride that he could recognize an opportunity and swiftly act. In this matter of the Vuelta Ranch, much more had happened than he had anticipated. Carruthers, the young Englishman, had traveled into Mexico and vanished. Without doubt he was dead. How dead, or why, did not matter. Only that he was dead. The sister, taken by Comanches, could be counted as dead. In full charge of the huge Vuelta Ranch now was a mere foreman named Pete Wilcox. The nearest owners now were far away in England, complete strangers to New Mexico. British money had been poured into the ranch and waited there now without owners to protect it.

Roddan's pulses were ticking faster as the facts ran through his mind. In a long lifetime a man might never again meet such an opportunity. A kind of excited elation put warmth in Roddan's smile. "There's another job for you, Cultus, at better pay."

The narrowing look Cultus gave him was not enthusiastic. "What kind of job?"

"Another bet to start with: two hundred dollars says you can't get a bunkhouse job at the ranch which Carruthers and his sister owned. Five hundred more says you'll not carry out any ideas I may have."

"You and your damn bets! Why don't you just make me an offer?"

149

Roddan's smile broadened. "I like to bet. When I lose, I pay."

"So far you have."

"Let's understand each other, Cultus." The smile lingered, hardening. "I'm making money. Each year I'm a little more important in the Territory. I help people who help me." Cold finality turned the lingering smile frosty. "We'd better both decide just where you stand in my plans."

"Where you need me, ain't that plain enough by now?"

"I wanted to hear it. Don't go to the ranch with guns hung under your armpits. Wear one gun in an open holster like any bunkhouse hand. If you meet anyone you know, say you went broke gambling and have to work."

"I'm back to cowhand then, just waiting for word from you."

"That's right."

Simon Roddan was whistling softly again between his teeth as he watched the man leave. Jack Cultus could kill a man impersonally and efficiently. He could handle a card deck with the best. He never drank too much and remained a coldly watchful man. But his essentially shallow mind failed to grasp the fact that a man who made a simple and careless bet could truthfully swear in court that he'd neither issued an order to kill, say, nor suggested that a killing be done. And, whatever the bet, it must be won before money changed hands. All guilt lay completely with the man who won the bet.

A practical man, Simon Roddan had learned early in life that only two important things existed: money and power. Equally early in life he had decided that he would have both. When he had won the Vuelta Grant in a bitter court contest, and had sold the Grant to the Englishman, he had needed the money for other schemes. The Vuelta at that time had been wild, undeveloped land, needing a small fortune invested before it could possibly be a paying proposition. The money, British money, had been put into the property. The Vuelta now held a solid promise of becoming one of the fabulously great ranches in the Territory. And the Vuelta, its owners far away, waited in brief uncertainty for the first man strong enough and clever enough and unscrupulous enough to seize it.

Because of the Vuelta Ranch, Judge Colin Bassett was not sleeping too well these nights. Old Zeke Winn's information about Geoffrey Carruthers and Ann Carruthers had brought suddenly and vividly to Bassett the massive responsibility he had agreed to on behalf of the bank. He had not shared Zeke Winn's far-fetched idea that Ann Carruthers might still be alive, and might possibly be ransomed by the Comancheros, who traded with the Indians far out on the plains of Texas. Young women simply did not come back from captivity with the Comanches or Kiowas. If not immediately violated to the point of death, they were quickly taken into some warrior's blankets and had children and growing shame so deep they did not usually welcome ransom. There seemed little doubt that Geoffrey Carruthers had died. Equally reasonably, one might consider Ann Carruthers as dead. No one knew better than Colin Bassett how the young Englishman had planned to develop the Vuelta. Or how much money and effort already had been put into the ranch. Ann Carruthers had left her instructions. If she disappeared, the bank was to wait sixty days and notify the family in England. And then what . . . ?

Colin Bassett was pondering the matter again, and weighing the ethics of certain personal thoughts when he turned a corner of the plaza and noticed the gambler and gunman, Jack Cultus, leaving the office of Simon Roddan. Some mysteries were immediately cleared up. Now Bassett knew who had sent Jack Cultus following Ann Carruthers to La Mesilla and on south. Roddan, always devious and coldly practical, must know that the Vuelta had lost its owners. And he would use that fact for his own profit, as he always did. Colin Bassett felt a sudden twinge of helplessness. Confined to his Santa Fe bank, with an immense responsibility now, he suspected that trouble was coming fast to the Vuelta Ranch. But he had no idea what would happen or what to do about it.

Don Emilio Martinez, of the plaza of Puerto de Luna on the Rio Pecos, rode ahead of his wagons, east, toward the Llano Estacado of Texas, as he had many times through the long years since he was a young man. Now Don Emilio's grandchildren were older than he had been when he first rode from the New Mexican settlements onto the vast plains of Texas. In these years of dignity and prosperity, Don Emilio Martinez was a tall, wide-shouldered old man with a white, patriarchal beard and a deep cello voice. The coat and pants he wore were of the softest, well-worked doeskin, and there was no finer rifle on the Plains than the long-barreled, heavy Sharp's across his saddle.

The wagons and two-wheeled, axle-squealing carretas were his property. The horses, oxen, and mules belonged to him. Many of the men were his sons and grandsons and cousins who would, God willing, have another fat year of prosperity when this trading with the Comanches, the Kiowas, Apaches and Cheyennes was over. For Don Emilio was the greatest of the Comancheros, those adventurous men from the settlements of New

Mexico who traveled far out on the Plains to trade with the Indians.

It had not always been so. Don Emilio could remember his first venture long ago of one lean burro pack of cheap trade trinkets he had exchanged for eight scrawny Texas steers and three horses, which then were riches indeed to a young *pelado*. Now he was Don Emilio, *majordomo* of all the Comancheros, whose heavy carretas were squealing and groaning as they rolled east to the Plains. With the dignity of his position, Don Emilio was courteous to the stranger whose horse came up from the rear at a long lope and pulled down to the same slow walk.

"God be with you, *Señor*."

"And with you, Don Emilio Martinez — long life and *mil* blessings. Together with the *salud* of friendship and respect from my *patrón*, Don Alfredo Correon de Leon y Delgado, of the Hacienda of Our Lady of Sorrows, in Chihuahua."

"Who," said Don Emilio, "does not know of that great man, Don Alfredo de Leon y Delgado, of the hacienda of so much magnificence? One is honored to hear his name at such distance."

"Not only his name, Don Emilio — but a letter from my *patrón*. I am Capitán Sanchez, who was a boy with Don Alfredo, and is trusted above all on the hacienda."

Don Emilio looked keenly, curiously at the stocky man with the gray-sprinkled mustache and hard, efficient look under the wide-brimmed, high-crowned straw hat. He took the letter sealed with red wax and wrapped in oiled silk, which Sanchez brought from a saddlebag.

"You have knowledge of what this letter says?"

"Yes, Don Emilio. My *patrón* informs you that I speak his mind and his thoughts. His honor is with me."

Still holding the letter unopened, Don Emilio turned

153

in the saddle. His cello-like voice boomed to the rear. "Fabien!"

"And what does the honor of Don Alfredo Delgado do so far away from his hacienda?" Don Emilio asked with mild irony.

"It has to do with twenty thousand silver pesos."

"Truly a rich honor." The young man who galloped up from the rear was bright-eyed, eager as Don Emilio handed him the letter. "What does it say, Fabien?"

The young man broke the two red wax seals and opened the missive. "It is from Don Alfredo Correon. . . ."

"Yes, yes, boy, of that I know. What does Don Alfredo Delgado have to say?"

"This man who brings the letter, Capitán Jorge Sanchez, speaks for Don Alfredo Delgado, his mind, his thoughts. . . ."

"And his honor, also?"

"*Si* . . . honor."

"Capitán Sanchez speaks only truth, and so we welcome him, Fabien. You will say it to all the others."

"Oh, *si, patrón.*"

When the youth had left them, Don Emilio, not at all abashed that he had not the facility of reading, said, "We will now let the honor of Don Alfredo speak further of twenty thousand silver pesos."

"It is a little matter of three *gringo* heads."

Don Emilio listened closely, and commented with more irony, "The heads, if found and taken, must be packed in salt and delivered to the Hacienda of Our Lady of Sorrows where Don Alfredo, like the paymaster of the devil, waits with the blood money."

"He will pay, *Señor.*"

"That is to be seen. And I am not in the head-collecting business. Those are Comanche and Apache tricks, with which I have no interest."

"My *patrón* wishes only that the Comancheros and Indians hear of this offer. Knowing that all men respect Don Emilio Martinez, he directed that the business be placed at your feet, for whatever profit might be made of it."

"He weaves a wide web, Capitán Sanchez. The price of a head on these plains is less than five and ten thousand silver pesos!"

"As God wills your wish, Don Emilio. Who takes the heads and what is paid does not matter. My *patrón* will pay as his honor states."

"I have not liking for the *gringos*. Nor have I hate. But silver pesos I understand. Five hundred silver pesos will buy land on these plains. You know the look of these three heads?"

"In my sleep, Don Emilio."

"For the heads which you agree are the ones desired, I will pay at my wagon camp two hundred silver pesos, in cash or trade. You may tell all that it is so, and I will call the good God to witness if I am asked. You are satisfied with that?"

"For my *patrón, mil gracias,* Don Emilio. Your wish is our wish."

Sanchez had expected something like this. Don Alfredo had warned him how it would be. "Listen, Sanchez, that old bull, Martinez, is the *majordomo* of all the thieves and rascals who sell guns and ammunition to the Comanches, Kiowas and Apaches, so they can come at our throats, killing and stealing for the profit of Don Martinez and his like. Kiss his hand and foot, if needed, for nothing else can be done without his good will, and everything can be done if his greed is stroked right. With that old rascal agreeable, all the Indians and the other thieves and

155

killers will be looking for the heads of these three *gringos*. They are with the Comanches now . . . and they will die as I have sworn. Into your hands, Sanchez. Find old Emilio Martinez, stroke his back and his thieve's pride." And now, all over the Plains the word would spread and men would be looking for the heads of the three *gringos*.

Chapter Sixteen

Layer by layer civilization, as they knew it, was being stripped away. That thought came again to Hardisty long before the Rio Grande was crossed. For him and for O'Meara, of course, the long ordeal on the water wheels and their escape had been a descent into brutishness. Ann Carruthers's real ordeal started in the quick, savage ambush in the mountain pass, and afterwards. Pale and anguished over the death of her brother, Ann had to watch in the fast-deepening twilight while the Comanches scalped, stripped and mutilated the dead hacienda guards.

In thin anguish, Ann said, "We can't leave Geoffrey to that."

Hardisty reassured her. "Juanito says there's a shovel in some of the stuff looted from the hacienda last night. O'Meara's gone with him to get it. We'll bury your brother decently before we leave with the Indians."

"With them?"

"We aren't safe in Mexico without them. You saw what almost happened to us."

Ann said distractedly, "It's all an unending nightmare!"

She was nearing hysteria. Hardisty spoke roughly to her, for her own good. "You're going to see women and children from the hacienda who are prisoners. You'll hear them crying and begging for help. And you won't be able to do a thing. Any hope you give them will be a

157

lie. But you're alive. You're not a prisoner. Are you going to be a hand-wringing, sniveling nuisance? A danger to all of us? Or a woman with some control?"

"I don't snivel," said Ann tightly and coldly, under full control again. "But I do dislike and despise people who deserve it. Remember that, Mr. Hardisty."

"You'll keep me reminded," Hardisty made a wry guess.

So in the new night they buried Geoffrey Carruthers and hurriedly piled rocks on the mounded dirt of the pitifully shallow grave. And went on.

There was nothing of a retreat about it, but the Comanches were traveling fast and well into the night, after hours of resting and waiting in the pass. And there were even more of them than Hardisty had suspected. The loosely-herded stolen horses, groups of warriors, scattered captives and packhorses carrying loot and food were strung out for miles. It was a tribute to Juan Tomás, Hardisty rightly guessed, that so many had come together for the huge raid. A Comanche war chief was only as strong as the men who followed him. For generations the Comanches had been raiding deep into Old Mexico, but only a chief like Juan Tomás could gather this many warriors together.

By the next day it became apparent that the Comanches and their more treacherous allies, the Kiowas, for the most part regarded them as white strangers with scalps and horses, guns, and women to be taken. The barrel-chested Juan Tomás was blunt about it.

"Hard'sty, I am frien' so I tell you this: stay close to me or Juanito. You understan'?"

Hardisty thought he understood, but he wanted to hear it. "Why must I stay close?"

"All close. Your wives, too."

"Why?"

"We lose many men an' do not take all the hacienda like I tell my people. Many say now, 'Why we have so little an' these white men so much? Even womans.' Two wives you have, Hard'sty. So I tell you, stay close. Is not good away."

Hardisty wanted to argue the matter because it was important. His plans had seemed simple enough. After they crossed the Rio Grande and the risk of pursuit by Delgado's men seemed over, he had hoped to strike north and west toward New Mexico. If they could find a stagecoach westbound from the Texas settlements to the Rio Grande settlements in New Mexico, most of their troubles would be over. Ann Carruthers could be started back to her ranch, to luxury and safety and whatever she desired. That would be the end of the Carruthers, brother and sister. And end any chance that Ann Carruthers might wish further help. Already the promise he'd made to Geoffrey Carruthers seemed distant and vaguely foolish. As for the young Mexican girl, Rosa Lopez, something could be done about her. Put her on a stagecoach at Paso del Norte, perhaps, with her passage paid south to Azul, and money enough to get her safely from Azul to the hacienda where she belonged.

But none of that would happen the way things seemed to be turning out. Hardisty argued with Juan Tomás, "You are a great war chief. With you we are safe."

"It is so."

"If men listen to Juan Tomás when we are with him, will they not listen when we are away?"

They were riding side by side. Juan Tomás had not donned a headpiece of buffalo horns or feathers. But the quill breastplate over his hide shirt was a richly worked thing. His carbine was in its boot. He was using a saddle with saddle horn, over which was looped shell belt and holstered revolver. But he carried his medicine shield, with its covering in place now, and his war lance with tufted scalps fluttering from the shaft. Three of the scalps were blond, but the hair was short — men's hair. Somehow that seemed to tell a little about this man who had so much white blood. He had killed white men and scalped them — but not white women.

A slight smile came under the bold nose, lighting the aquiline features. Tolerance filled the man's glance. "Long Bull is war chief. Walks-With-Wolf is war chief. Sankata, Quiet Owl, Running Wind, all war chiefs. They bring men to this fight an' listen to my voice. Now, quick they go. Men listen again to Walks-With-Wolf. To Sankata. Even now not to Juan Tomás!"

What it boiled down to, Hardisty saw clearly, was a little less than comforting. While the bright Comanche Moon of late summer flooded the vast prairies, the war chiefs had been out raiding. Juan Tomás had brought many of the chiefs and their men together for this raid into Old Mexico. During the raid his authority had been unquestioned. But now the huge raiding party was ready to splinter off into its parts. And what Juan Tomás could order his own men to do, would be ignored by Long Bull's men.

As long as they stayed with Juan Tomás and the men who followed him, their scalps were reasonably safe. That was some forty-odd men, Hardisty guessed. Away from Juan Tomás and those men, however, they were no safer than any sodbuster and his family caught helpless on the open prairie.

Thoughtfully, Hardisty dropped back and talked it over with O'Meara. "Alone," he decided, "we might make a ride for it and come out all right."

O'Meara grinned. "You ain't alone, laddie. You an'

your two wives'll be with Juan Tomás clean up through Texas until he lights at his home lodges. By then you'll be smellin' like Indians an' talkin Comanch' in your sleep."

"You," said Hardisty bluntly, "can slip off and keep going."

"Not me. A man who grabs hisself two wives in one night," said O'Meara with a smirk, "has bit off enough pure trouble to keep him chewin', chokin' and sweating. And I aim to stay close and watch."

"They're not my wives."

"There's a few score Comanches think they are. An' the way that Rosa Lopez takes on over you sure ain't makin' anyone think different," O'Meara said with amusement.

Hardisty shook his head. Rosa Lopez was unabashed womanhood. She had a man now and wanted only to serve him. Not that it was unpleasant to have a sultry-eyed girl consider herself his woman, body and soul. He was a man. His pulses could speed up when Rosa's flashing, provocative smile turned to him and the black lashes over brown, submissive eyes lidded tantalizingly.

Ann Carruthers, the older of the two girls, was coolly blunt about it. In her precise, school-learned Spanish, she said, "Rosa, you are young and pretty. But you will find much trouble offering yourself to a strange man this way."

"He is not strange man. What am I if he don't kill for me? Did he not tell these Indios I am his wife?"

"He was trying to protect us. After all, he . . . he said that same thing about me."

"What I care? When I am through with him, you are welcome to what is left."

"Rosa!"

"Hah! You are jealous because you are one cold Anglo woman. Me, I am hot-blood Mexican. You watch me. I will make my man happy. What will you do for him?"

Ann had reddened awkwardly.

O'Meara, making himself slyly helpful in Spanish, said, "Why don't you two wives fight over him? Winner gets him all week."

"Why I fight a cold Anglo woman who don't want a man?" Rosa said, shrugging scornfully.

Hardisty had slacked his horse back in time to hear part of it. "Listen, both of you," he said in Spanish which was all Rosa understood, "back at the hacienda I had to call each of you my wife to protect you. You saw it. You know it. The Indians were taking women for slaves. I still have to pretend you're my wives. And I don't like it any better than you do."

"I like it," Rosa corrected promptly.

"And you, Rosa . . . I'm not your man. Understand that?"

"Oh, *si, Señor Gringo,*" Rosa said meekly, provocative eyes flashing under her long lashes.

O'Meara chuckled. Hardisty had to grin. Rosa laughed delightedly. It was not possible to be angry with this lithe, spirited, uninhibited young Mexican girl.

An edged soberness hung over all, as if high hopes had not fully materialized. There was open haste, as if one project was over and abandoned and they were hurrying on to new ones. The fierce pace was jading horses, causing increasing suffering among the captives, making the two girls look thinner in the men's clothes that had belonged to the two dead hacienda guards. At night they collapsed under their thin, dirty blankets and had to be roughly shaken out in the cool dawn. Hardisty could only marvel that the two women did not yield more under the steady, merciless riding from pre-dawn to last light. Any horse that faltered or dropped was swiftly butchered for eating. Hardisty had never pushed horseflesh this hard before. He began to see why these magnificent riders of the plains were reputed to travel sixty, a hundred miles a day. How they could appear magically, vanish, then suddenly could be raiding, burning, killing at incredible distances away.

They crossed the Rio Grande and swung more directly north through a dry desolation of semi-desert covered with greasewood, amole, Spanish bayonet, thorny mesquite, and cactus. There were tanks, seeps, shallow waterholes — and the Comanches knew them all. They should know them, Hardisty reflected. In the old days, under the same bright Comanche Moon, their grandfathers had raided this way deep into Old Mexico. And had returned like this with horses, cattle, loot and helpless captives, mostly women and children. The women for concubines and slaves, the children to be reared as good Comanches and Kiowas.

Hardisty was firm about one thing. "You two ladies wait on me like wives," he told them both in Spanish. "Fix food for O'Meara and me. Serve us. Don't eat until we're eating. All that is woman's work. If we try any of it, we lose face among these Indians, and we can't take that chance. If they start laughing at us for squaw work, we're no protection for you."

"So we're merely squaws now?" Ann asked coldly.

O'Meara dropped his wild Irishman's sly levity over the matter of two wives for Hardisty. "That's what you are now . . . white squaws," O'Meara said soberly. "Hardisty's right, exactly right in what he says. All that these Indians understand is a woman acting like a squaw should act. Any man doing squaw work gets squaw treat-

163

ment from them."

Rosa was cheerful about it. "I make good squaw. I like to wait on my man."

Ann said stiffly, "Say exactly what you want done and we will do it. This is your show, you know." In such small ways she let him know her true feelings.

And a time never came when it could be said that the big raiding party was breaking up. Rather it was eroding. Without apparent planning, groups split off and vanished quickly over the horizon, usually east toward the Texas settlements. Finally there were only thirty-nine warriors left, all taking orders from Juan Tomás. As they now rode slower, halted earlier, and started later, there was a more relaxed feeling in the air.

Hardisty also noted something which pleased him at first. Juanito was spending more time with them. And this was a different man from the sullen and surly young Indian captive on the water wheels. Somewhere this Quahada Comanche had found doeskin leggins and a soft leather shirt worked with quills. His hair had been washed and freshly greased and now was its full lustrous brown. He had not donned war paint. The high, lean cheekbones and thin nostrils, the deeply-tanned skin almost as light, actually, as any white man's skin, brought out what was really so: this young man was not even half Quahada Comanche. His father had had a white mother. His own mother was white. He had more white blood than Indian blood, and Juanito seemed instinctively to be turning more and more to those whose blood was more like his own.

He had a debt to Hardisty and O'Meara, who had been prisoners with him and who had made possible his full freedom from the rusty wrist and leg shackles. As an Indian, he could have repaid that debt and felt free to scalp them later on. This was different. With more white blood than Indian, he seemed to find real pleasure in their company. He laughed and talked gaily with Ann Carruthers. And the English girl who spoke very little to Hardisty, and that usually unsmilingly, seemed to make a point of extra friendliness with Juanito.

The afternoon of the second day like that, one of the flankers, ranging far out and to the side, put a small, brief smoke on the horizon, and they turned that way.

Hardisty called to Juanito, "What did that smoke say?"

Juanito had been laughing with Ann. He answered lightly, "It say, 'Come to me.' I t'ink he find somet'ing."

A small apprehension touched Hardisty. "What would he find?"

Juanito shrugged. "We see."

They were riding at the rear, inconspicuous, which was Hardisty's idea. Now Juanito galloped ahead and, when the first strung-out riders halted and the others began to gather at the spot, Juanito galloped back to them.

"I t'ink is not good to see."

"What is it, Juanito?" Ann asked.

"Stagecoach."

Hardisty said coolly, "I want these women to see everything. It won't help them to keep their eyes closed."

Suspicion jumped into Juanito's stare. Challenge edged his demand. "What you mean, Hard'sty? What you tryin' do?"

Only the gratitude of this young Comanche and his father stood between them and disaster. This suspicion, this challenging Jaunito could be dangerous. Hardisty spoke diplomatically. "My wives, Juanito, are not children. They are women. Must women hide their eyes?"

"You like them hate Indians!"

It was said to Hardisty, but Juanito's eyes went to Ann

Carruthers. And this was the moment the first alarmed suspicion touched Hardisty. He suddenly wondered how he could have been blind and not have guessed what was happening.

"Juanito has been my friend," Hardisty said gravely. "Juan Tomás is my friend."

The challenge and suspicion slowly faded from the darkly handsome young face. Juanito nodded. "Is not good," he said gloomily, pointing ahead with his chin. "Sankata's men burn stagecoach. Juan Tomás never burn stagecoach."

No, Hardisty thought cynically, Juan Tomás is too smart for that. Burned stagecoaches bring Army troops and Texas Rangers. Aloud he said, "We will look." And to the girls, because he'd taken a stand on the matter, "You will see these things which Juan Tomás and Juanito do not do." And he thought, that's laying it on mighty thick. Would he swallow it?

Apparently so. Juanito's challenge did not return. He made no protest when Hardisty, the two girls, and O'Meara rode to the spot.

It had been a westbound stage with a six-horse hitch. Two horses had been shot at full run and had fallen in the harness. The other four horses had been cut out of the harness and driven away. The coach had been burned. A few embers still smoked. Five men had been killed. Two of them would be the driver and the shotgun guard. Three had been passengers. One was a young army officer.

There were no dead women — but there were two dead babies, each under a year old, each lanced to death and tossed into the flames. So there had been two young mothers and they were gone — alive. Captives. Were they still alive? Or wanting to live?

166

Luggage and mail bags had been dragged off the boot and slashed open. Windblown letters were scattered over the sparse bunch grass and dry earth. Male, female and infant clothing littered the ground.

This time Rosa Lopez was not sick. But she sat silently on her horse, eyes closed, gray pallor under her olive skin. Ann Carruthers stared at the sprawled, mutilated men and charred remains of the babies. Under the wide-brimmed Mexican hat and the desert tan deepening on her face day by day was taut, frozen-faced control.

A letter, face-up, caught Hardisty's eye. He bent and picked it up. In a bold hand was written, Anthony J. Mulholland, Esq., Las Cruces, New Mexico Territory.

Looking at the bodies, the burned stagecoach, the wind-stirred litter on the ground, it was easy to believe everything was savagery, brutality, death. But the simple address on this letter promised that the little-used ruts running out of sight east and west eventually reached cities and towns where men mailed and received letters in calm certainty that all was peaceful in their world. But did these same road ruts run west to gutted stage relay stations and more bodies? To Comanches, Apaches, raiding, killing?

"The bunch that did this," O'Meara said, "took off west toward the next relay station. Think it's worth the risk of heading that way?"

Hardisty's decision was reluctant. "Not with the two women along."

O'Meara was laconic. "My idea, too. If we didn't get jumped by Comanches, we probably would by Apaches. We're safe with this bunch until they hook up with the Comancheros and start trading."

Hardisty nodded. "From there we can get over into New Mexico without trouble."

167

The looted shovel from the hacienda had been taken by Comanches who had split off. There was no way to bury the dead, and no time to do it. When they rode on north, the frozen look remained on Ann Carruthers's face.

Miles farther on some of it wrenched out of her to Hardisty. "Those babies! Their mothers. . . !"

"That stagecoach should have had a military escort."

"We . . . we should be able to do something about those mothers."

"Meaning, O'Meara and myself should do something?"

"You're friendly with this Juan Tomás. Couldn't you ask him to go after those women and . . . and get them? I . . . I have money."

"You? Money? Here?"

"I brought money from Santa Fe in a money belt, which I am still wearing."

He said flatly, "It wouldn't work."

"You could try," Ann insisted with desperate resentment.

"Keep quiet about any money you have," Hardisty said sternly. "And get out of your mind that one Comanche war chief — especially one like Juan Tomás — would track down another war chief and haggle over captives. That goes on when the Comanchero trading starts. If those women are alive now, they've been badly used already, you can be sure."

"Something could be done. I'm sure of it."

"There are thirty-nine armed men in this bunch alone — and O'Meara and I are only two. And we've got two helpless women to worry about." Bitterness edged Hardisty's voice. "Stop expecting miracles. They won't happen. If we can get you two through alive and safe, we've done more than we think we can."

She was stiff. "I'm not ungrateful."

"No one wants your gratitude. But take this advice: stop being so friendly with these Comanches. Stay close to O'Meara and me, and let us do the talking."

"In other words, act like a squaw."

"That's exactly what you are now, as far as any of them know or care."

Flushed anger backed the look she gave him. "I'm not a squaw and never will be, Mister Hardisty. And if you are demanding that I stop being friendly with Juanito, I will not. You know that he's more than half-white . . . and he's starved for contact with his own kind. You can see it in the way his eyes light up when he talks to me."

Hardisty gave her a disgusted stare. "I've warned you," he said curtly. "Since you're my squaw as far as any of them know, I could beat you, and they'd laugh at your screams and think you were getting exactly what you deserved . . . which you would be."

"You would beat me?" asked Ann furiously.

"Of course not," said Hardisty coldly. "Why should I care that much about what happens to a hard-headed female? I've warned you, now you do what you like."

"I shall!"

She welcomed Juanito with a warm smile when he dropped back and rode with them. She laughed often while the two of them talked. She was eager, interested. And, as she was obviously trying to do, she brought out a side of the young Indian that Hardisty might not have guessed existed. The quiet reserve of Comanche heritage vanished when Juanito was riding side-by-side with Ann. He talked more, laughed oftener, and emotions flashed over his face in swift play of light and shadow.

O'Meara watched it. "She's buildin' trouble," he warned from the corner of his mouth. "Can't you get sense into her head?"

"I warned her. The trouble will be hers."

"He thinks she's your squaw. Could be your trouble. Big trouble."

Hardisty nodded. "If it happens, I'll have to do what I can."

"Women!" O'Meara said irritably under his breath.

They were traveling slower now. At times, half and more of the Indians were ranging out of sight east, west, ahead. Twice Juanito vanished most of a day. Noting the hours men disappeared and the condition of their ponies when they returned, Hardisty guessed that, while their advance headed steadily north, a strip of prairie sixty to eighty miles wide was being kept under observation.

He told O'Meara, "They're looking for something . . . a wagon train, maybe."

"Can't be settlers this far out on the plains."

"A trail herd," Hardisty settled on a guess. "They're not bringing back as much from Mexico as they planned. If they can take cattle to the Comancheros for trading, they'll do well. And through here is where cattle head for the Horsehead Crossing and north up the Pecos."

O'Meara spat to one side expressively. "Laddie, what do we do if these Indios jump a trail herd?"

"Nothing."

"Good Texas men slaughtered under our noses?"

"We can do nothing."

"I dunno. Wouldn't be like Delgado's hacienda being jumped and us being helped by it. It'd be like we watched cold-bloodedly while that stagecoach was jumped an' burned."

170

"Exactly what we'd have had to do . . . what we will have to do. One move against this bunch now and we get shot and the girls taken."

"I could ride out ahead and warn any herd I find." When Hardisty's eyebrows lifted, O'Meara growled, "I could try."

"And do how much good? The crew with the trail herd would still have to fight. Out this far on the plains, they already know what to expect."

"But doin' nothin'. . . ."

"Men are watching every move you make," Hardisty reminded. "Even if you slipped away at night, the girls would be in danger from sunrise on."

O'Meara muttered, "Always it comes back to the girls."

"Doesn't it?"

Chapter Seventeen

Hours before it happened, they knew what was going to happen. One of the flanking riders far over the horizon had sighted victims. A rider came in at full gallop and spoke excitedly to Juan Tomás. And now, once more, Hardisty saw a war chief in action. There was no huddle of talk. Juan Tomás gave brief orders. Other riders lined out across the prairie. Juanito dropped back, smiling delightedly.

"What is happening?" Ann asked him.

"We take cattle. Many cattle." He was eager, exuberant.

"A trail herd?" Hardisty asked.

"Yes."

Ann visibly swallowed. "A trail herd is going to be attacked?"

"We will have many cattle to trade."

"They're not your cattle, Juanito."

His arm made a wide sweep. "All this belong my people. This Comanche land. We take." When he spoke to Hardisty, the smile was gone. He was curt, "This time Juanito tell you keep women here. Juan Tomás say so."

Ann pleaded, "Juanito. . . ."

He wheeled his horse by the single jaw rein and rode forward, ignoring her.

Hardisty murmured wickedly, "This is the other side

of it — the Indian side."

"They're going to kill innocent men. He's going to help them. . . ."

"Not exactly helpless men," Hardisty told her. "They'll be armed. They know what to expect."

"And once more you won't do anything?"

She could push a man to the edge. With an effort, Hardisty held his temper. "Not a thing. It's between the crew of that trail herd and Juan Tomás, who's had plenty of practice at this sort of thing."

He watched keenly every move that was being made. The flankers and the men who had gone after them began to ride in. Smoke could have called them in — but smoke, Hardisty guessed, would also have alarmed the crew with the trail herd.

Hard-ridden horses were exchanged for fresh ones. Medicine shield covers were removed. Rifles were checked. Warriors stripped to breech-clouts and tied up the tails of their ponies. And when they finally rode off, only six men were left with the horse herd, and pack horses, and mules. The Indians rode northeast, growing smaller in the distance, dipping down out of sight and reappearing.

"They'll try to surprise that crew," Hardisty guessed to O'Meara.

And O'Meara struck his fist on the saddle horn.

"Should be a way to warn 'em!"

"There isn't . . . unless you and me get killed and these girls get turned into Comanche slaves. Want that?"

"You know damn well I don't."

"Then sweat it out."

Not until hours later did they learn what had happened. The half-defeat at the Delgado hacienda was not a true measure of Juan Tomás. The trail herd was medium small,

173

some eight hundred head of gaunt, bony Texas steers. A rickety chuck wagon was drawn by six oxen. The crew numbered only seven, including the cook, a bald-headed man with a fringe of white hair. Two of the meager crew were not long past boyhood. Hardisty learned such things later, from Juanito and Juan Tomás, and from personal inspection.

Two of the crew were riding point at the head of the strung-out herd. Two were midway back in the swing position. Two were at the rear in the dust of the stragglers and drags. The sun-warped, creaking old chuck wagon was lumbering at the rear, well back out of the dust of the drags.

Juan Tomás stationed his men in a long depression in the prairie and waited patiently. The first third of the Comanches waited until the old chuck wagon was abreast of them and not far away, and burst out at it in full silent gallop. They were almost to the wagon before the bald-headed driver sighted them. He was shot off the seat. The wagon was cut off from herd and crew, and any chance of using it for a fort was gone.

Already the main body of Comanches was a long line of whooping, screaming danger thundering at the herd and its small crew. Nervous steers stampeded toward the north, sweeping along the point and swing men on that side. The two men with the drag were already facing the Indians who had taken the chuck wagon. That left two men to face the furious charge of over twenty Comanches. One was shot as he tried to use his rifle. The other one went with the stampede in a wild ride to escape. Three men of the crew eventually escaped. And when the stampede ran itself out in the north, that was merely the new direction the herd would be taking anyway.

The astuteness of Juan Tomás was brought home to

Hardisty by the fate of the chuck wagon. It was not burned, not looted or wrecked. The six lumbering oxen in the wagon yokes were not injured. When the stampede was over, the scattered cattle and remuda were close-herded again. The chuck wagon was brought up for use. The three men who had escaped were not followed.

And that was the day in which Juanito took another scalp. It was tied at his belt when Hardisty saw him, and there was no doubt he was a young warrior who brought pride to Juan Tomás.

O'Meara was helplessly angry as they moved on north across the Texas prairie with the looted trail herd. "Them clabberheads shoulda' known better'n to bring a trail herd this way with a measly crew of seven."

"They took a chance on getting through," Hardisty guessed. "If they could have made the Horsehead Crossing and gotten up the Pecos far enough, they could have driven as far as Montana, to good range and markets. A few days earlier or later and these Comanches would have missed them. They might have gotten through safely."

"A whole trail herd lost an' four good men dead. . . ," O'Meara lapsed into scowling silence before a thought cheered him slightly. "Them three who got away might bring help back an' bust this business wide open."

"D'you think so?"

"No," O'Meara confessed. "This herd an' remuda, an' all the horses brought outa Mexico, will be pushed north for trading with the Comancheros. And that is where we take off on our own. Happy day it'll be."

"Juanito told Ann that part of the men are going to take the horses and push on ahead. The cattle can come on slower."

"They won't get there too fast for me." O'Meara was

175

silent for a moment; then he was sourly blunt, "That girl keeps getting thicker with that young Indian. You better stop her."

"She's stubborn."

"She's picked the wrong time, the wrong man, the wrong place to be stubborn."

"I think so, too."

"She's supposed to be your squaw. Handle her!"

"If she's going to be bull-headed, it's her deal."

"Just don't forget," warned O'Meara, "that all the protection we got is the good will of this young buck an' his old man. Let that girl bust it up with her foolishness an' there'll be more fat burning than we can handle."

"I know," was all Hardisty could say.

Still, the next afternoon, he was startled when the matter came to a sudden head. The large herd of horses was a full mile ahead of the trail herd. To escape dust, Hardisty, O'Meara and the two girls were riding leisurely between the horses and cattle. There seemed no particular meaning when Juan Tomás rode back at a slow trot, greeted Hardisty with a palm chest high, and wheeled in beside him.

The aquiline features with high cheekbones, bold nose, stern mouth, had not a great deal of expression, but that was usual. Once more Hardisty was struck by the fact that here was a great war chief of the Quahada Comanches who was half-white and looked it. And again he wondered if the white blood and the Indian blood clashed inside the man. And if so, how much.

"You are well, Hard'sty?"

"I am well, Juan Tomás. You are well?"

"I am well." Silence followed, until Juan Tomás spoke again. "Tomorrow I take horses north. You go?"

"We'll go with you."

Silence fell again. The distant bawling of steers drifted up from the rear. And once more Juan Tomás spoke, with almost a white man's bluntness.

"Hard'sty does not take one wife into his blanket. She smiled upon Juanito. For this woman he will pay one hundred horses, one hundred cattle."

Hardisty thought, Here it comes! Why didn't I beat her and stop it? Now it might be too late. He said, "This woman has brought me luck. You understand?"

"Yes."

If he said the wrong things now, they might decide to take both girls. The seriousness of all this was evident from the fantastic price Juanito was offering. At the same time, Hardisty was suddenly sorry for the young man, for this Juanito, more white by heritage than Indian. Something deep, instinctive must be reaching out to a girl like Ann. Yet any wife Juanito took would never be more than a squaw. There was some hope, because this was being done in the formal way.

"I will do this the white man's way. I will let this woman know that Juanito wants to take her to the blanket — and has offered many horses and steers for her."

Juan Tomás nodded and lifted his rein to ride ahead. Hardisty stopped him.

"I want Juan Tomás to hear what I say, and what the woman says to me."

A keen, quick look appraised his face. The chief's nod was grave.

Hardisty called over, "Ann! Come here, please!"

She rode over, putting her horse between their horses as Hardisty indicated. Her smile at Juan Tomás was ignored and faded as she looked curiously at Hardisty.

"Juanito," Hardisty said clearly and deliberately, "has taken a liking to you. Through his father, he is offering a hundred horses and a hundred steers for you."

Red rushed into Ann's face. She looked to see if this were humor and realized it was not. "H-horses and s-steers for me?"

"A high price. Far more than a Comanche woman or a captured slave woman would bring."

"I. . . ." The flush was draining away, leaving strain, pallor. Words seemed to be clogging in Ann's throat.

"In his eyes, you're used goods," Hardisty told her. "But he's still willing to make you his squaw."

Ann whispered, "You can't mean this!"

"Juan Tomás? Do I speak truth to this woman?"

"You speak truth, Hard'sty."

"This," Hardisty said coldly to her, "is not London or Denver or Santa Fe, where you can flirt with a man and walk away. Here you're only a squaw belonging to me. When you smile at another man, you give him ideas he can only think are right. Juan Tomás is an honorable man in this. He will see that you are bought in an honorable way, and the son will treat you well."

Ann sounded thinly hysterical. "You talk as if you were considering making such a sale."

"It's my right. If you were not my squaw, Juanito could have taken you days ago. You are my squaw, aren't you?"

Ann Carruthers gave him a shocked, resentful look. She swallowed. "I. . . ." She swallowed again. "Yes . . . I am your squaw," she said in a low voice.

"I told Juan Tomás I would handle this in the white man's way," said Hardisty, still coldly. "I'll let you decide what is to be done, but I want Juan Tomás to hear what is said."

She was angry and she was frightened, because she knew that this could happen.

178

"It is my decision?" Ann asked thinly.

"Yes."

"I . . . Juanito has made a mistake. I . . . thought he was your friend and so he was my . . . my friend. I am your . . . your squaw and do not want any other man. . . ."

"You have heard, Juan Tomás?" Hardisty said.

"I have heard. The white blood in Juanito calls to white blood. He has seen that this woman has a warm heart and has seemed cold to her man. He will wait." A lifted hand, and Juan Tomás heeled his horse into a trot toward the horse herd well ahead of them.

"Juanito will wait?" The thin edge of hysteria was in her voice again.

"He thinks you may change your mind. He sees how you treat your man and how you treat Juanito. What else can he think?"

O'Meara brought his horse over. Rosa Lopez was siding him. "Everything all right?" he asked.

"Juanito wants to buy Ann. His father made an offer of a hundred horses and a hundred steers."

O'Meara's whistle was softly amazed. "I never heard of any woman bringing that price. He means business. What'll happen?"

"They don't really think they can buy me?" Ann was outraged, indignant. "Like . . . like a mare! A cow!"

"They can buy you or take you," O'Meara assured her. "Hardisty and I seen this coming. Wasn't a way to head it off, bull-headed as you been actin'. Everyone could see you smilin' wider at the Indian than at Hardisty. And Hardisty was your man. You were his squaw."

"I wasn't a squaw!" The edge of hysteria was back in her voice again, accusing Hardisty. "You made it my decision . . . as if it didn't matter whether the man

179

bought me or not!"

His shrug was unmoved. "I promised your brother I'd do what I could to help you. Calling you my wife, so the Indians would let you alone, was part of it. You haven't liked the idea. And you've almost run yourself into a Comanche blanket and a lifetime with the tribe."

"What can I do?"

"Act like a wife who's satisfied with her man. And keep away from other men. If this is headed right, you may get out of it. If Juanito and his father are made to look like fools in this, they may just take you. I'm doing what I can to stop this, but you'll have to help me."

"You . . . you promised Geoffrey to help me?"

"Yes."

"He . . . Geoffrey wanted you to help me?"

"Yes."

After the death of her brother she had drawn back into a shell of reserved, inner grief, not even speaking of him. Now she said, "Then Geoffrey did trust you . . . completely."

"He could have been wrong."

Ann shook her head. "Not where I was concerned." And in a low voice she said, "No one told me."

That was her last reference to the matter. But Hardisty sensed that a barrier had been breached. If her brother had trusted him, she also would trust him completely. At bedtime that night she showed it matter-of-factly and without false modesty. She brought her blanket beside Hardisty's blanket.

"If they must have evidence that I am satisfied with a man, they shall have it," Ann said calmly. Wrapped in her blanket, she was directly beside him, at his left.

"Good girl," Hardisty said.

Rosa Lopez brought her blanket defiantly to Hardisty's other side and rolled in it. Since with a scant, dirty blanket apiece they slept in their clothes, there was little of significance about it. Even Hardisty had to grin slightly when O'Meara, off to the side, chuckled.

"Big chief with his squaws close," O'Meara said in Spanish, so Rosa would understand.

The Mexican girl now knew of the offer Juanito had made. Close at Hardisty's right side she said in Spanish, "This Juanito is nice young man, *Señor Gringo*. I think she like him very much when you sell her."

"Not going to sell her, Rosa."

"Why not?"

"She doesn't want to be sold."

"Why you care? She don't like you. She like him. Me, I am here. I am your woman. I show you. Any time I show you, *Señor Gringo*. I am much woman."

Gazing up at the stars at Hardisty's left, her high-crowned sombrero on the earth at her head, Ann said calmly, "Go to sleep, Rosa, and I'll be right here when you wake up."

The small buffalo chip fire had lost its last glow and the late moon had not yet risen when his hair-trigger sense of danger brought Hardisty wide awake. A stealthy arm had touched him.

He was tensing to reach for the revolver rolled in the blanket with him when he became aware that his left shoulder was supporting the head of a sound sleeper, and her arm was across his chest. Not stealthily as alarm would have cried, but slackly, naturally, in sound sleep. Hardisty lay very still, looking up at the cold, bright stars. On his other side Rosa had turned her back to him and was sleeping soundly. O'Meara was audibly snoring.

181

Ann was breathing lightly. She seemed utterly relaxed and trusting. Tendrils of her hair were against his cheek; the scent of her hair was in his nostrils. His left arm could have slipped under her shoulders and drawn her closer, and he was tempted.

Instead he listened to her soft breathing and the sounds of the night. Far toward the horizon the howl of a loafer wolf drifted to the stars. Rosa moaned softly in her sleep and jerked slightly from some disturbed dream. Ann shuddered; her arm held him tighter and her head burrowed more comfortably into his shoulder.

It seemed a long time to Hardisty that he lay like that without moving, while Ann slept trustfully. And when she did awake, it must have been as abruptly as his own awakening had been. He heard her slight gasp of dismay. Her head lifted from his shoulder, her arm lifted from his chest. He sensed that she was peering at his face. Eyes closed, he was breathing evenly in apparent sleep. It was some moments before Ann turned away and relaxed. He believed she was still awake when he slept again.

In the morning Ann gave him an uncertain, wary look, when he said, "This is the day, I think, when we go on ahead with the horses."

She seemed relieved at his casual manner, and said equally as casually, "I hope so."

In the second hour of the morning, Juan Tomás, riding forward from the stolen trail herd, paused with them again.

"You are well, Hard'sty?"

"I am well. You are well, Juan Tomás?"

"*Si*." The Indian was terse. "Horses go now to *Cañon del Mejicanos*. You go?"

"Yes."

"Juanito go with cattle."

"So?"

"You don' sell woman?"

"You heard her say."

"I have heard. Juanito will wait."

There was no moment of abrupt, hurried departure. Gradually the large horse herd was pushed into a slow, mile-eating trot which began to draw ahead. By midday the plodding cattle had dropped back over the horizon and were seen no more in the vast sweep of undulating, short-grass prairie.

O'Meara said, "He said we're headin' for the Canyon of the Mexicans? Where's that?"

Hardisty shrugged. "I've heard of several places where the Comancheros meet the Indians, the Palo Duro, the *Cañon del Rescate,* and one called The Valley of Tears because so many captive women and children are brought there, and split up and traded around. There are other places, but I don't know them all."

"Any of them'll do," O'Meara guessed. "As soon as we get with New Mexico traders, we can stop worrying."

Hardisty's nod agreed.

Chapter Eighteen

Don Emilio Martinez knew that the Indians called it the Canyon of the Mexicans. The savages were welcome to call it anything they chose. To Don Emilio it was 'The Canyon', which in reality meant 'My Canyon.' Here, where the yellow and brown and red canyon walls soared up hundreds of feet to the caprock standing bold and rugged against the sky, he had come with his first pack mule and few cheap trade trinkets.

Here every year since then he had come back and back and back with his ever-increasing stock of trade goods. No matter where else he went to trade in the course of the year, here was always the first and longest stop. And the Indios knew it, and came here and waited here.

In this sunny mid-morning, in front of his tent by his wagons and two-wheeled carretas, Don Emilio sat comfortably in an old Army canvas chair, fingering his patriarchal white beard, and looked up and down the great canyon he liked to think of as his own. Seep springs made cool pools along the base of the cliffs and gave life and glinting current to the small creek which threaded among cottonwoods, wild China trees, and hackberry, and past mottes of gnarled cedars. Mile upon mile of sheltered, grassy canyon and rippling creek along which buffalo hide lodges and brush ramadas and wickiups of Kiowas and

Cheyennes, Comanches and Apaches stretched out of sight.

And in brush ramadas and crude adobe huts, in tents, wagons and beside open air burro packs were other traders. But of them all Don Emilio Martinez was the oldest, richest, most powerful and respected trader.

Inside the loose oval formed by his wagons, carretas, and tents, on long strips of canvas, were set out his gourds and bottles of wines and whiskies, and lengths of colored cloths. There were knives and beads, pistols and lead, muskets and ammunition. Hungry eyes could find axes and threads, needles, tin buckets, shirts, petticoats, skirts, and various breads, cookies, candies, mirrors. All the articles that a long lifetime had shown that the savages of the plains and mountains, the warriors, squaws and children, would be eager to have.

With pleasure Don Emilio watched the choicest of his grandsons, slender young Fabien Martinez, ride in from the lower canyon at a trail lope and dismount in front of the canvas chair and say respectfully, *"Buenos dias, Señor."*

"Ho, young pup, what bone hast thou uncovered to make the eyes so eager?"

"Juan Tomás has come to his lodges with many horses, and many cattle are following."

"On his head, benedictions. No greater thief rides the plains. You will take Anton Chico wine to Juan Tomás, with the friendship of the Martinez family."

"How many bottles, *Señor?*"

"One bottle, foolish pup. A man who is drunk will trade with anyone, forgetting his friends."

"He has brought horses with the three crosses branded on the left hip."

"Eh?"

185

"The Triple Cross of the Hacienda of Our Lady of Sorrows, *Señor*. As the Capitán Sanchez said."

"So! An old man forgets. Or possibly does not wish to think of such things. So Juan Tomás has been stealing in Chihuahua?"

"*Si, señor.*"

"And there is more to this big bone you gnaw? Three men with him, perhaps?"

"Two, *Señor*. Two *gringo* men and two women. Is the salt ready, *Señor?*"

"There was no talk of women by this Sanchez. And I do not like this matter of silver pesos for heads to be delivered in salt."

"It is a kind of trade we have not done, *Señor*. But profitable."

"Perhaps, thou innocent. What kind of man will hire his killing done?"

"Wise man, *Señor?*"

"Too wise, perhaps, for young pups. When the killing has been done, who will recognize that head in a sack of salt? That black, drying head which even its own mother would not know?"

"But upon the honor of this. . . ."

A calm snort cut that off. "Honor is honor . . . and silver pesos are silver pesos," the calm, cello-like voice of Don Emilio admonished. "When a man is dead, why pay for his killing? The dead will not live again. And if a mistake has been made, if the head does not look right. . . ?"

"He would not dare!"

"On his hacienda, in Chihuahua?" Don Emilio shook his head sadly. "Oh, pup of my heart, there is so much to . Attention. I give you this order."

" ."

"Not a word of this to the Capitán Sanchez. We will wait and watch. Not a word to anyone."

Fabien smiled sheepishly. "Not a word," he promised.

The first thing Hardisty did in the Canyon of the Mexicans was borrow fourteen gold coins from one of the fat little pockets of Ann Carruthers's money belt.

"Take more," Ann urged.

"I think this is too much."

He left the weathered, hide-covered teepee which would be their home for several days and rode up the canyon in search of a trader. Already he knew much about this *Cañon del Mejicanos*. While warriors were out raiding, many lodges were moved here into the canyon to wait for the horses, cattle, loot, and even captives, which could be traded. Hardisty already knew that tens of thousands of horses and cattle had been brought into New Mexico by the Comanchero traders, and thousands more would be moved in this season. Now he was witnessing what happened.

The lodges of Juan Tomás's Quahada Comanches had been waiting in the lower canyon, and there had been quick joy over the loot and wailing grief for dead warriors who would not return. Other tribes were scattered up and down the canyon. Some war parties were still out. Others already had returned. The chief trader was a white-bearded, old New Mexican named Martinez, but there were other, smaller traders.

It was from one such trader at a rickety, canvas-covered wagon that Hardisty managed to buy a red neckerchief, a mirror, a comb, a cake of soap, two towels, scissors, and a pair of trousers and a shirt. He could have bought more with good yellow gold, and knew he bargained carelessly, but he was hurried.

187

The trousers of sky-blue kersey cloth had the yellow cavalry stripes down the outer seams of the legs. The shirt of heavy gray flannel and the trousers, too, he suspected, had been stolen from some Army post. But they fit him and would do here. When he looked into the mirror, his grunt was rueful. No wonder Ann Carruthers had suspected he was a ruffian. A man who looked like that would have to be!

There had been a keen razor in one of the saddlebags captured from the hacienda guards. Hardisty rode downstream from the Quahada Comanche lodges until he found a willow thicket by the water, which formed a partial screen, at least. First, with the mirror dangling from a willow twig, he shaved all the tough, prickly beard. And then snipped off some of the tangled hair. After that he stripped and lathered from hair to feet.

Even the comb and towel were luxuries. The sky blue pants and gray shirt were a snug fit. His long damp hair combed out smoothly, the red bandanna kerchief made a splash of color at his neck. Shell belt and revolver settled reassuringly at his waist. He was John Hardisty again, wolfish-lean, utterly tough and hard now but with a cavalryman's dash over it, so that he was passable, at least, once more.

He left the old ripped shirt and filthy, worn-out pants there on the stream bank, and rode back to the teepee. When he stepped inside, Ann Carruthers gasped and jumped to her feet. "What do you mean coming. . . ." She broke off, staring speechlessly. "I thought it was a stranger . . . you . . . you. . . ." A flush started at her neck and moved up into her cheeks. "You look . . . different," Ann finished lamely.

Hardisty grinned. "Hope so. I looked in the mirror before I shaved. It was bad." He had wrapped the small mirror, comb, and soap in the second towel, and gave them to her now. "I was hoping you'd cut more of my hair."

Ann nodded and indicated the earthen floor of the lodge. "Sit down."

On her knees beside him, she used comb and scissors as if cutting a man's hair skillfully were habitual with her. "I often trimmed Geoffrey's hair." Then, in a low voice, she said, "I . . . I can't accept that he'll never be at the ranch again."

"Will you stay on at the ranch?"

"Oh, yes. Geoffrey would expect it." Ann moved behind him, scissors snipping busily. "Almost all that both of us had, and borrowed money also, has gone into the ranch," she said matter-of-factly. "There's not much chance of getting the money out by selling."

"Not a chance," Hardisty agreed.

"So I must go back and make it a profitable ranch," Ann said in the same matter-of-fact tone. Her question, moments later, was serious. "Is this really the end of our trouble?"

"It could be," was all Hardisty would admit. "We'll rest here several days, buy what we need, and leave. O'Meara will go as far as your ranch, in case he's needed."

"I'll be most grateful. And . . . and hope I can make it up to him in some way." Ann was silent for several moments. "What will you do about Rosa?"

"She should go back to the hacienda."

"She can hardly do that. She doesn't want to. And, after all, she is your responsibility. You can't discard her where she knows no one."

"I don't know what to do with her."

"You may have to marry her, really."

"I've thought about that. She's . . . Ouch. . . !" Wincing,

Hardisty put fingers to the side of his head. "You almost pulled that tangle of hair out by the roots."

"I'm so sorry," Ann said coolly, and didn't sound as if she were sorry at all.

Minutes later the scissors paused again when, without warning, Rosa Lopez burst into the lodge. Rosa's eyes were wide, terrified. She had been running. Shuddering breaths choked off the words she tried to utter.

Chapter Nineteen

Hardisty had lunged to his feet and looked swiftly outside. Quiet peace was all he saw. Ann was on her feet also, scissors forgotten in her hand.

"Rosa! Has someone hurt you?" Ann demanded in Spanish. "What happened?"

"*Am'rilla. . . ,*" Rosa gasped. "*¡Amarilla!*" It meant 'yellow,' and when Rosa gulped another breath, she got the rest of it out. "Yellow Hairs . . . here!"

Hardisty broke in roughly in Spanish, "Yellow Hairs from the hacienda? Here?"

"*¡Si!*"

"How many?"

"Capitán Sanchez!"

"Who else?"

Rosa's shrug was frightened. She was recovering breath. "I see this one man on a horse and I hide. . . ."

"Where was he?"

Ann put her arm around the shaken girl. "What were you doing? What happened?"

Rosa calmed somewhat. She had walked to the other end of the Comanche encampment, and had talked to an Indian girl about her age who knew a few words of Spanish. Both girls had gone into a lodge where the girl's mother was sewing on a moccasin. When Rosa had stepped out again, she had seen the strange man on a horse skirting the Comanche lodges. Recognizing Capitán Sanchez she had stepped back into the lodge, and not until the man was out of sight had she run here in panic. She had seen only the one man.

Hardisty asked, "Was he wearing the yellow, spotted vest?"

"No, *Señor Gringo.*"

"Did he see you?"

"No."

"How far away? Which way was he riding?"

The rider had been at least a hundred yards away. Rosa had seen only his profile before she ducked back out of sight in panic.

"Couldn't it have been another man?"

"I don't think so."

"You're sure not?"

"Is possible," Rosa admitted.

Hardisty grinned tolerantly at her. "If Yellow Hairs were here," he pointed out, "there would be fighting. And why would this Sanchez — a man I know — come this far into Texas alone?"

"I think," said Rosa, "he come to take me back."

By now even Ann was smiling.

"I don't think that would happen," Ann said lightly. "But since you're afraid, Rosa, don't go out until the men have made certain no one from the hacienda is here."

"I'll have a look," Hardisty decided.

His horse was waiting outside the lodge, a chunky, powerful bay which had belonged to one of the hacienda guards. He had a rifle in a saddle scabbard, revolver at his hip, clean gray shirt and sky blue pants which fitted. He was clean shaven and his hair had been trimmed. He felt light-hearted and human for the first time since his first day on the hacienda water wheels.

But he had no illusions about this canyon of the Comancheros, or the Comancheros themselves, or the Indians they traded with. Too well now he knew the savage cruelty and violence which made possible all this trading. The Indians could be accepted for what they were — savages born to violence and wanting little else. But the men who traded with them were little better. Without this Comanchero trade, much of the killing would never happen. These Comanchero markets for horses and cattle, and the guns and ammunition traded to the Indians, kept much of the long frontier aflame year after year.

Hardisty was also coolly sensible. There was nothing he could do about any of it. And to Juan Tomás and Juanito, and the Indians who took their orders, he owed life and safety now for O'Meara, himself, and the two girls. A precarious safety, at that, for he never knew each day whether another day would be the same.

It was late afternoon when he rode slowly up the canyon. O'Meara was probably somewhere ahead, looking around, also. This Canyon of the Mexicans, Hardisty decided, more truthfully should have been called the Canyon of the Indians, for here the Indians without doubt were supreme. They swaggered; they rode their ponies proudly. Armed warriors far outnumbered the native New Mexico traders, mixed breeds, and scatter of rascally-looking Anglo traders. The Comancheros could have been wiped out at any time, but they were the only suppliers of powder and ball, cartridges, rifles, revolvers. And liquors. Here, Hardisty reflected, was the one spot on all the frontier where the greater the rascal, the greater the safety.

Shadows were beginning to crawl out across the canyon floor, although hundreds of feet overhead the caprock looked clear and hot in the blaze of the late afternoon sun. He rode past Kiowas and Cheyennes, and recognized chunky Apaches. Mescalero Apaches, he guessed, for they were the Apache tribe nearest to the plains. There was, obviously, visiting back and forth between the Indians, and trading with one another.

"Hey, you — mister!"

To the left of the shallow little creek, in a thin scattering of cottonwoods, was an adobe shack with a canvas-sheeted wagon alongside.

The man who stood in front of the shack had a square-chopped beard and shirtsleeves rolled up. Hands cupped at his mouth, he called again, "You Hardisty?"

"Yes."

"O'Meara's here — drunker'n a boiled coot! Better come get 'im."

Resignedly Hardisty wheeled his horse splashing across the shallow little stream. O'Meara, wild Irishman that he was, certainly was the man to get into something like this as quickly as possible. He sighted O'Meara's horse behind the wagon, with two other horses. And when he rode closer and saw the slabby face, shifty fish eyes, square, tobacco-stained yellow beard of the man who had shouted, annoyance at O'Meara stirred.

There was not much choice of company in a place like this. But O'Meara could have done better than this lanky ruffian with a gun on his hip who lived beside clean water and preferred to stay dirty. A man who had trade goods, including whiskey, obviously, and who wore pants and shirt that were stiffly slick with grease, food droppings and dirt.

Hardisty reined up in front of the shack. It had, he noted idly, a brush roof, adobe back and ends, and half the front was open, without door or windows. On planks across boxes inside was a scanty stock of trade goods.

He called, "O'Meara?"

"Wastin' breath, mister. He's on the dirt, cold. Wilson, me partner in there, was tryin' to bring 'im around when I seen you."

"It'll be wild trade whiskey if it dropped O'Meara like that, and serves him right for hogging it down." Hardisty was dismounting. He dropped the reins. "If O'Meara was out cold, how'd you know who I was?" a thought made him ask the slab-faced rascal who was showing snag teeth in a slack grin.

"He was talkin' about you. Said you was down the canyon with them Comanch's. When you come riding, I took a chance an' hollered."

The man was still talking when Hardisty stepped into the open front of the shack. The floor was pounded dirt. O'Meara, over to the right, was stretched full length on the earth. The bulking, pot-bellied figure by O'Meara would be the partner, Wilson. And, if it were possible, this Wilson was even more unprepossessing.

At some time in his life, Wilson had been a large, square-shouldered, powerful man. The outlines were still there, blurred by the sagging pot belly, porcine jowls, huge, moon-like face and fat, grimy hands. This Wilson had a heavy brown mustache, but the rest of his face had not been shaved in many days, and coat and pants were soiled and greasy, too.

Wilson wheezed, "Tried to wake him but he wouldn't move. Might be you have better luck."

In the end of the shack here the shadows were deeper. Wilson's eyes sunk in folds of fat had a dull shine of virtue. The smell of bad whiskey hung rankly. And something nagged at the back of Hardisty's mind as he bent over O'Meara. Something he should know and couldn't recall. Something that was important. Suddenly he got it.

"Did O'Meara spend all his money?" Hardisty asked casually.

Behind him the lanky, slab-faced man said, "He drunk up all he had, an' more on credit."

Their money — all their money — had been taken from them at the hacienda in Mexico. Their pockets had been empty. O'Meara hadn't borrowed from Ann Carruthers. She had told Hardisty to tell O'Meara when he came back that he could borrow from her money belt. O'Meara hadn't any money to buy whiskey.

Now, bending over O'Meara, Hardisty suddenly saw two things: blood smeared on O'Meara's right ear and Wilson's feet making a sudden shift of movement toward him. His lunge away from the big man was instinctive and barely enough. The knife blade barely missed his back and slashed viciously through the left sleeve of his new gray flannel shirt.

The lunge carried him stumbling over O'Meara and crashing into planks holding trade goods. He drove on against the toppling planks to escape the next knife slash that would surely follow. O'Meara was probably dead. Wilson and the square-bearded partner blocked escape.

Rage such as he had not known in a long time exploded in Hardisty's brain as planks and trade goods clattered to the floor and he snatched for the revolver holstered at his hip.

"Stop him, Wilse!"

When Hardisty wheeled back, the knife had lifted to strike again and the quivering mass of the fat man was surging at him. There was no time to draw the gun. The holster was not tied down. He swiveled the holster up and shot through the bottom — square into the massive fat belly — and fired again as he ducked to the right away from the collapsing bulk pitching forward and down.

It ploughed into the debris of planks and scrambled trade goods and heaved in clumsy shock.

All of it had happened in seconds. The slab-faced man was backing away, drawing a revolver as Hardisty yanked his own gun free. The man shot first, wildly, fast, and missed. Hardisty's first bullet struck his hip and spun him off balance. He staggered, one leg useless, and fell, losing his gun from a nerveless hand.

His gasp was thin. "Don't kill me!"

Panting, Hardisty stepped back and caught up the dropped gun. "If O'Meara's dead," he promised viciously, "you're dead, too!"

"He ain't! Wilse only laid him out with a ax handle!"

"Why?"

"Old Emilio Martinez is payin' two hundred dollars for each of you dead! If'n we didn't get it, some'n else would! You done smashed my hip! I won't never walk agin'!"

"You can crawl then."

Blood was running down Hardisty's left arm and dripping in a red spatter off his fingertips. He looked at the upper arm where the new shirt had been slashed. Under it the flesh had been laid open for inches. But there was no pumping artery blood and the arm would still move with strength. He saw blue and red cotton bandannas in the mess of trade goods knocked to the floor and grabbed up a handful, stuffing some in his hip pocket for later, and using several as a pad to press over the bleeding gash.

He had holstered his own revolver and shoved the other gun inside his pants belt, and now he knelt by O'Meara and pushed his hand inside O'Meara's shirt. The slow, even beat of the Irishman's heart helped him relax a little. He was rough but thorough as his right fingers dug into

O'Meara's scalp, and found only a lump and a scalp gash and not a shattered bullet hole. And there was no outward sign on O'Meara of a deep cut by the vicious skinning knife the fat man had wielded.

Holding the pad of bandannas over his left arm again, Hardisty stood up. The fat man was breathing in choking gasps now, not moving. He was going to die, and quickly, Hardisty guessed. The other one would probably live, but be crippled, and that was his worry. He was lucky if he were allowed to live.

"Who is this Emilio Martinez?" Hardisty demanded.

"Biggest trader in the canyon, biggest on the plains."

"Why does he want us dead?"

"Dunno."

"How did he know we were here?"

"Dunno. He offered the money fer three Anglo men who might come in with Comanch'. An' you two come."

"Three men?"

"Uh-huh. I'm dyin!"

"You'll probably live," Hardisty said without sympathy. "Your kind usually does. One more thing. Did this Emilio Martinez offer any money for a woman dead?"

"Wasn't no talk about a woman."

O'Meara groaned softly and moved an arm. Hardisty was kneeling beside him when O'Meara stirred and opened his eyes.

"A man," said Hardisty, "who scrabbles around with hogs, gets up a hog. And only a thick-headed Irishman would be dumb enough to do it."

"Say no more. I'm rememberin' I was drinkin' when me lights went out." O'Meara struggled to a sitting position, looking blearily around. "The scuts was givin' me whiskey that went down like snake heads an' tacks. Faith, was it a fight I started?"

"You started nothing, and got your thick noodle cracked with an ax handle. Can you get up and climb on your horse?"

O'Meara got groggily to his feet. Vision was clearing as he looked around at the shambles, at the fat man still gasping and dying slowly, at the other groaning man, at Hardisty's bloody left arm.

"Holy cow!"

"They meant to kill us both. Get on your horse."

"What about these two?"

"Indians or other traders will be along."

"This man's bleedin'!"

"He can crawl over and get some cloth and try to stop it. I'll explain."

They left the slab-faced man cursing them thickly, and turned their horses down the canyon toward the Comanche lodges. In curt words Hardisty told what had happened.

"I was riding this way when they hailed me an' offered me a bottle," O'Meara said.

"And your throat cut if I hadn't come along. You were good bait for me. We're worth two hundred a head, paid at this damn Martinez wagon, evidently."

"Ain't an Indian or trader wouldn't shoot us for two hundred silver dollars!"

"That's right."

"It don't make sense. We don't know this Martinez."

"It's happening, and there's some sense shaping to it." Hardisty told about Rosa's belief that she had seen Capitán Sanchez, from Mexico. "And it was Sanchez she saw. That's the only thing that'll explain money offered for three men killed. Only someone from Mexico could bring word that three of us got away, and might be with the Comanches who drifted in here to trade."

"To this God-forsaken canyon out in Texas? Hell!" O'Meara spat. "Why'd Delgado go to that trouble after we got away? And how'd anyone get here ahead of us?"

"A man could do it by fast stage north from Azul and Paso del Norte, and fast riding to this Comanchero country. That was Sanchez prowling around the Comanche camp, looking for white men or horses with the Triple Cross brand of the hacienda."

"But why? He won't get them damn horses back! It ain't helpin' anything to have us killed now."

"Maybe Delgado wanted Carruthers dead because of the Vuelta Ranch. And you and me dead because we weren't too polite before we left. And maybe the three of us meant trouble over chaining men to those damn water wheels. Something like that could make a stink between London, Washington, and Mexico City."

"Cut it any way you like," O'Meara summed it up, "there's a bounty on our heads big enough to make every Comanchero and Indian in the canyon take after our hair."

"Exactly, with shots in the back, or any way they can drop us fast and without a chance."

"So what do we do?"

"I want the girls to know what has happened if we're killed. Then we'll call on this Martinez. And hope we run into Sanchez. There's only one way to stop a bounty on your head, stop the man who's offering it."

In the weathered Comanche lodge which was all the home the four of them had now, Ann caught breath at sight of Hardisty's arm. He grinned at her and offered the new bandannas dangling from his hip pocket.

"The bleeding's about stopped. If you could bandage me a little. . . . And Rosa did see Sanchez." He was brutally blunt in describing exactly what they were all facing. "You've seen what the Indians will do. These Comancheros will do as much for money. Delgado, back in Mexico, seemed to be offering the money."

Ann was calm. "Could it have anything to do with my Vuelta Ranch?"

"It could. O'Meara and I will try to find out. You girls stay out of sight."

"And if you're not back?"

"I don't know the answer to that," Hardisty admitted honestly.

Chapter Twenty

In all men linger primitive urges from the ancient years, the driving flame of sex, the naked bite of hunger. But the animal sense of danger lurks deepest and strongest. And as Hardisty and O'Meara rode up the canyon in the fast-thickening twilight, danger sharpened every primitive sense of survival.

Scent. Hardisty caught himself sniffing wood smoke from cook fires which lay in low, thin blue layers this time of day. Sight. Each figure, each child or squaw, each man afoot or on horseback, was weighed and judged. Sound. Dogs barking, voices calling, the trot of a horse nearby with an Indian on the bare back, were marked safe or possibly dangerous. And the one man he and O'Meara looked for most keenly was the man who had come out of Mexico fast with the gift of death — Sanchez.

They did not see Sanchez.

In exploring up the canyon, O'Meara had sighted the Martinez corral of wagons, carretas and tents.

"A half-breed said this old Emilio Martinez will trade for cattle and horses here in the canyon and start 'em to New Mexico," O'Meara said. "Then Martinez will head on toward the Palo Duro country for more trading."

The first night shadows were clotting in the canyon bottom before they found the Martinez camp on a sprawling flat near the base of the cliff. Open cook fires toward

202

the rear were casting circles of light and spewing up little fountains of sparks. The wagons and two-wheeled carretas, well separated, with tents in between, formed a sizable oval. Back by the fires a man was playing a guitar and singing. He sounded gay, carefree. Quite a few men seemed to be around the fires. They had been brought, Hardisty suspected, to drive cattle and horses back to New Mexico.

A man riding in from the upper canyon greeted them. *"Buenos noches, Señores."*

"Speak English?" Hardisty asked.

"Sure thing." The man — he was young — reined up, chuckling. "You want something?"

"Where can I find Emilio Martinez?"

"In that first tent where the lantern is lighted inside."

"Thanks."

When they were alone, O'Meara said, "Ain't that handy. Right out in front, waiting for us!"

"I'll do the talking," Hardisty decided. "You wait near the tent. Watch for trouble, but don't start it."

O'Meara dismounted and held the horses. Hardisty's steps were almost soundless on the earth as he pulled up the tent flap and ducked inside, gun in hand.

The lantern was hanging from the ridge pole. There was a cot. And in canvas chairs two men were sitting with glasses and cigars in their hands. On a small table between them was a box of cigars and a bottle.

Blinking in the light, Hardisty demanded, "Which one is Martinez?"

The wide-shouldered old man with a patriarchal beard looked placidly at the gun.

"If you want money, *Señor,* there is none in this tent. If trouble, I am only a peaceful trader."

Hardisty's smile was thin. "You're a liar, at least."

The other one, short and bony, with a white mustache and ragged chin beard, opened his mouth in silent laughter. This man's face had a dark, parchment hue from the long years spent in the open. His words lacked the subtle Mexican background accent.

"You've met him some'eres, 'Milio. Sounds like he knows you from who danced the turkey."

"Martinez," Hardisty said curtly, "look at my left arm. I'm one of the men worth two hundred a head . . . dead. Two of your men tried to collect. How much d'you think you're worth alive now?"

The smaller man chuckled. "I'd say a short two-bits. 'Milio, I knowed you'd get greedy enough to bite a scorpion tail. And this'n has got a real stinger."

In a cello-like voice, Martinez calmly asked, "Was a man killed?"

"One of your men. Maybe two."

Martinez opened big, blue-veined hands expressively.

"Not my men, *Señor*. They have all been told I have regretted making the offer."

"Why did you make it?"

"For three heads delivered to Mexico, I was offered thousands of silver pesos."

"By Sanchez?"

"Who spoke for his *patrón*." Martinez remained placid. "If you are one of the men, you left enemies in Mexico, *Señor*. I am only a trader, and decided not to deal in salted heads, which had to be delivered to Mexico for payment."

"Those who shake hands with the devil, catch hell," Hardisty said equally calmly, and completely cold now. "We'll go to the Comanche camp. In the morning, we'll start for the Vuelta Ranch, near Canimongo, New Mexico. You'll guide us and, if there's trouble from anyone in the canyon, there'll be a gun at your back."

Hardisty had the peculiar feeling that neither old man paid much attention to what he said. Their eyes had quickly sought each other with an unspoken message. The smaller man spoke calmly, seriously now. "Son, have you seen a young lady named Carruthers?"

"Yes."

"She with the Comanch's?"

"Yes."

"They harmed her?"

"No."

"A ol' has-been like me, son, ain't a danger to no one. Lemme go to that Comanch' camp and see her."

"Why?"

"I know her."

"What's your name?"

"Zeke Winn."

"Zeke Winn?" This could be the old mountain man. Age and size fitted. "Where did you see her last?"

"Dammit! At the Delgado hacienda in Chihuahua just afore the damned Comanch's jumped the place. I was outside the house. When it was over, she was gone. Delgado said she'd took a walk outside, too. I come from Santa Fe to here, hopin' fer some trace of her when the Comanch' bands started coming in to trade."

That was good enough. Hardisty asked, "How far can I trust Martinez?"

"You can't. But 'Milio and me been brushin' together nigh forty years. If he tells you you're safe, you are."

Martinez was slowly stroking the full white beard. In the lantern light his eyes were beginning to glint with something like humor.

"Put up your gun, *Señor*. I am too old a man to be taken as a guide to New Mexico. They would laugh at me from the Rio Grande to the Palo Duro. My *compadre* will guide you."

"This Sanchez? Where can I find him?"

A big, gnarled hand waved carelessly, "There is no need for a killing. All men in the canyon will be told that you are my friend. That will be good enough. You have other worries, *Señor,* if you have feelings for this *señorita,* of whom we were talking when you came in. She has much trouble she does not know about."

"What else has happened?"

Zeke Winn drained his glass, knocked ash from his cigar, and stood up.

"On the way here I camped one night with a stranger. He'd worked on the Vuelta Ranch an' quit when gun hands were moved in. Seems both the Vuelta owners was dead. The foreman was killed in an argument with a man he'd hired. The new owner sent in gun hands like he expected trouble, put in his own foreman, an' took charge."

"Who claims to be the new owner?"

"Man named Simon Roddan."

"Don't know him."

"Roddan sold the Vuelta Grant to Miss Carruthers an' her brother. Now he's took it back an' got gun hands holding it. You heered anything about her brother?"

"He's dead. I promised him I'd help his sister with the ranch if she needed help."

"I think," said Zeke Winn coolly, "we got talkin' to do, fast."

Five of them, trail-toughened, knowing that even days might count now, traveled from the *Cañon del Mejicanos* in Texas to the Vuelta country in New Mexico Territory. But first the blunt truth had been examined before they left the hide-covered lodge in the Comanche camp. Hardisty put it into words that night in the Comanche lodge. Two candles were burning — O'Meara and himself, Zeke Winn, Ann Carruthers, and even Rosa Lopez, who could not understand their English but had been told briefly what had happened, had been present.

"Seems fairly plain," Hardisty said, after hearing all Zeke Winn and Ann knew. "This Simon Roddan got the Vuelta Grant from the Delgado family in a nasty court fight where forged documents, perjury, and outright theft were alleged by the losing side. Some of it may have been true and some not. But Simon Roddan won the verdict.

"Also, there's no doubt that Ann and her brother were trailed to Paso del Norte and Azul by this gunman and cheap gambler Zeke Winn says is named Jack Cultus. Seems no doubt now that Simon Roddan sent him . . . which meant that Roddan was scheming, even then.

"We know that Geoffrey Carruthers had just vanished, leaving no trace, because we were there with him. We know from Zeke Winn that Ann was thought dead, or at least it was assumed she would never return. So it's plain that this Simon Roddan suddenly was certain that the Vuelta Ranch had no owners. It was waiting there, an immense and valuable property, to be scooped up by anyone who established some sort of ownership first. And since he'd gotten the property once, it must have seemed logical he could get it back with all improvements.

"The ranch foreman, Pete Wilcox, was killed. We can guess that was planned. Gunmen have been hired for the ranch crew. That serves notice that Simon Roddan has moved in with little more than squatter's rights and intends to hold the ranch with guns."

Ann's voice was low and bitter.

"Won't the courts protect me?" She added, "In Great Britain they would."

"This will be New Mexico. The law will often be what a man makes it. A court suit might take years. Meanwhile, Roddan would occupy the ranch. He'll have some shred of so-called proof that he has a right to hold the ranch."

"In other words," Ann said with increased bitterness, "a woman leaves her property for some weeks . . . and it is stolen from her."

"Usually that wouldn't happen. But when owners disappear and are thought dead, it opens the gate for thieves to move in. Simon Roddan moved. Fast. And from what Zeke Winn says, Roddan is no common thief. He is a clever, dangerous man, willing to gamble for high stakes. And in this case, the gamble must have seemed easy. The owners had vanished. With a little quick ruthlessness, a big bluff and guns put quickly on the ranch to back him up, he had everything suddenly in his pocket."

"What can I do?" Ann asked. In the wavering candlelight she looked pale, strained, as they sat on the floor of the Comanche lodge.

"You can let him have the ranch or fight him."

"You know I will fight him!"

"Good," Hardisty said. "You can't wait for the courts to act. Roddan moved fast. You'll have to move fast. In your own way."

"You mean hire gunmen?"

"He'd just out-hire you, two to one. And have the advantage of already holding the ranch. But he knows he's a thief. He thinks you are dead. If you return alive, he can't be sure that your brother is not also alive, and also moving against him. And the brother will be out of his sight, where he can't reach him. Roddan's guilt

208

will have to face things he can see and things he can't see. And he doesn't know that O'Meara, myself, and Zeke Winn, know you. Now, my idea is this. . . ."

Chapter Twenty-One

Through the window of the ranch office, in the rear corner of the sprawling new house, Simon Roddan saw another stranger being brought in. That was an order: any man caught on the ranch was brought to the house. Harmless men were escorted off the ranch. Usually they were glad to go for their treatment was never gentle. Roddan wanted ruthlessness to hang about ranch and crew like a warning pall.

This sun-drenched afternoon he had been working at the desk, whistling softly. He had never felt better. Every plan was breaking right. He was, Simon Roddan knew by now, one of the rare men who were always successful. During the late war he had carefully planned the future. Here in New Mexico Territory every plan was working out. Wealth and influence were growing. And this great Vuelta Ranch promised to be one of the capstones of his career.

Even Roddan hadn't realized how much sound British money had been poured almost recklessly into the ranch. And he had it all now, for nothing! Who else would have sensed that here was a ranch without owners? Who else would have taken possession so swiftly and ruthlessly? The old saying was true: possession is most points of the law.

The office door opening into the ranch yard was open.

Roddan stood on the bottom of the three steps outside and watched the stranger and his guard dismount. Several of the armed ranch crew were drifting over from the horse corral to watch.

The stranger had a bay horse and a sorrel pack horse. An almost black-tanned, muscle-and-bone man with bleached brows making slashes above his eyes, he wore brown wool pants, blue shirt and jacket, shell belt and revolver, and a carbine filled the saddle scabbard. Conroy, a dark-browed, wide-faced man with scowl wrinkles and surly lines at his thick mouth had brought the man in.

"He was headin' toward the house," Conroy said.

"On the ranch road?"

"Yes."

Roddan could almost guess what was coming. "Got a name, stranger?"

The man dusted his black hat against his leg. "Hardisty," he said briefly, and turned a level look at Conroy who had stepped up and prodded him nearer the steps with a carbine muzzle.

"Your business on the Vuelta?" Roddan demanded brusquely. At times like this he was never friendly.

Hardisty's shrug was casual. "Passing through. In that town — Canimongo — I heard that a man might hire here at good wages."

"Passing through from where?"

"Texas."

Roddan was deliberately curt. "What makes you think you're worth good wages?"

Hardisty jerked his head at Conroy and the three men who were watching. "They worth it?"

"They're drawing the wages, at least."

"Watch."

Hardisty was turning as he spoke. His left hand slapped

the carbine muzzle aside. He stepped in closer. His right fist lashed under Conroy's instinctive up-flung arm and drove in deep above the man's gunbelt. The gasp driven out of Conroy was explosive. He bent forward, sick, nerveless for a moment. Almost lazily now — but fast — Hardisty drew his belt gun and chopped the barrel neatly to the man's head. Conroy collapsed like an axed steer.

Hardisty backed off where he could watch the office steps and Roddan, also. His gun was covering the three men.

"Want to help him?" he asked coldly.

Not one of the three did, Roddan noted with a stir of anger. They were looking at Conroy without pity or much interest. Their wages were high, but they were a miserable lot in Roddan's estimation. The best he could do on short notice. With time, he meant to weed out and replace, and eventually have all the men as good as this Hardisty seemed to be.

"Move into the bunkhouse," he told Hardisty. "If Conroy wants trouble, handle him any way you please. There's no place on this ranch for weaklings."

"Kill him?"

"If he forces it. The foreman is Jack Cultus. Don't eye his job, even if you think you can shoot faster, which I doubt. Cultus stays foreman."

"Good enough," Hardisty said coolly.

Three days ago he had split off from the others and headed to Canimongo. In another day, O'Meara would split off. Old Zeke Winn would guide Ann Carruthers and Rosa Lopez to Las Vegas, the last important town on the Santa Fe trail before Santa Fe. Ann had promised to look after the young Mexican girl. The stage would bring the two girls from Las Vegas to Canimongo.

212

Zeke Winn had not been certain what he would do. "I been over ever' foot of the Vuelta Grant in the old days," Zeke had said. "Ain't no reason why I can't look it over again. Folks don't pay much mind any more to a ol' has-been like me."

The horses they had brought out of Mexico, with the hacienda Triple Cross brand, had been traded to the Comancheros for horses with Texas brands. With Ann's money, they had bought supplies and clothing, and had left for New Mexico.

Now Hardisty was on the Vuelta Ranch, inside Simon Roddan's guard. He had guessed it might be possible because there was no way Roddan could suspect this stranger had any connection with Ann Carruthers. And the ranch needed tough men.

As he led his two horses to the corral, Hardisty smiled slightly at a thought. Even one worm could quickly rot an apple. He was the first worm in Simon Roddan's new shining apple that was the Vuelta Ranch.

The only sullen enmity seemed to be from Conroy, the man he had buffaloed. In the first hour, in front of the bunkhouse, Hardisty was curtly blunt about it.

"You want trouble, feel free," he told the scowling Conroy.

"You had no call to come at me that way."

"Did you think you could keep jabbing me in the back with a rifle? Don't ever point a gun my way and we'll get along."

Conroy spat and walked away, the surly lines around his mouth deeper. But Hardisty had given public warning, and it was taken that way by the other men who heard. They would repeat it, Hardisty knew.

Jack Cultus, the foreman, was the only member of the old ranch crew that was left. Roddan had brought in his own men. So many of them that a long storage shed had been turned into a second bunkhouse. Nine men were at the ranch house that first day. Other men, Hardisty quickly learned, were at line cabins and patrolling the ranch, and changing Carruthers's horse and cattle brands to Simon Roddan's Diamond 48 brand.

There was a sense of urgency, of haste in the air, and wary watchfulness and suspicion. Men Hardisty spoke to did not seem quite clear as to why all this was happening. Simon Roddan, they knew, had taken over this huge ranch and wanted no outsiders on it. The men were hired to meet trouble if it happened. That was all they knew.

Hardisty decided he must be the only man on the ranch outside of Roddan and his foreman who knew what was happening and why. He was the only other man who could guess with cold clarity the meaning of every move being made. He knew that the owners had vanished and the huge ranch had been brazenly taken over by Simon Roddan. He knew now that Jack Cultus was the man who had killed the former foreman and was the same man who had traced Ann Carruthers and her brother south into Mexico.

Now all trace of the former owners was being wiped out as quickly as possible. The old crew was gone. The cattle and horse brands were being vented and changed. Anyone who might dispute what was happening was barred from the ranch. Strangers who might carry tales to the outside world were not allowed inside the ranch boundaries for more than an hour or so. Just enough time to question them closely and hustle them out. Any legal moves which possible heirs might make at some future time would take place in distant courts, against evidence that Simon Roddan would present. He was a lawyer. He was accustomed to using the courts to further his plans. He would have evidence of some kind which would be hard to refute. And he would have solid possession.

Cultus, the foreman, was a muscular, flat-faced man with high cheek bones, a tight mouth under a black mustache touched with gray. One look when Cultus rode in from a branding camp on the second day and Hardisty knew the type. Cultus was a gunman first, and after that a so-so ranch foreman, not greatly interested in cattle or horses.

On the fifth day, Roddan, with wagon and driver and six armed riders, went into Canimongo for supplies and mail. Seven armed riders returned. O'Meara was the seventh man, hired in town. And now, Hardisty told himself with cool satisfaction, there were two worms in Roddan's apple.

He and O'Meara were not in the same bunkhouse. Their stares were blank when they passed. And yet it was a warming thought to know that the big, lusty Irishman was close again.

Hardisty was studying the crew, the ranch routine, and the ranch itself. It was sobering to realize that the mile upon endless mile of range and mountains belonged to Ann Carruthers. South and east of the ranch house the land rolled like a vast, down-sweeping park dotted with green junipers and an occasional thicket of larger cedars. North and east, long wooded ridges called the Porcupines, with grassy valleys between, thrust out from the first soaring ramparts of the Red Mountains. To the west and north the higher benches and rising forested and grassy slopes of the Reds were gashed by dark canyons.

Colorado Creek and Frio Creek brawled down out of the high country. There were seeps, arroyos, washes which had water at various times during the year. The worst of the winter storms were broken by the mountains and ridges. There was winter graze to the south and east, summer graze in the high country, and deer, bear, wild sheep, turkey, mountain lions, high up. And Ann Carruthers owned it all and it had been stolen from her.

Chapter Twenty-Two

In some lives, once at least, comes a moment of shattering shock when the brain numbs, knees weaken, and the dismaying helplessness of childhood comes for a second, or longer. It happened to Simon Roddan in mid-afternoon as he stood near the corral talking to Jack Cultus. He had believed himself a man of hard purpose who had met danger and laughed, who often had dared greatly and remained calm. But when the two-horse buggy came fast around the end of the house, past the office window, and drew up at the office steps, Simon Roddan went speechless, numb in brain and body.

The dark-browed, surly Conroy had been riding fast to keep close to the racing buggy. "She wouldn't pay no attention to me!" Conroy called in baffled irritation.

Ann Carruthers was in the buggy, which had been rented, Roddan saw, from the town livery. His mind numbed under the shock. The girl was dead, or should be a broken Comanche slave, repeatedly raped. Yet here she was, pert, stylish in a small hat and close-fitting blue dress, and tanned, assured, and haughty.

"Mr. Roddan! Perhaps you can say why this strange man should try to give me orders as I drive on my own property!"

This couldn't be happening. Walking toward the

217

buggy, Roddan said inanely, "Perhaps he didn't know who you were."

"Why should he know who I am? He isn't one of my crew. I don't see anyone who belongs on this ranch. Including you, Mr. Roddan!"

Throat constricted, hat forgotten in his hand, Roddan halted beside the buggy. "Been changes . . . if . . . if you'll come into the office, I'll explain."

She was coldly informal now, "Obviously many things need explaining."

"Hold the buggy horses," Roddan snapped at Conroy.

Ann Carruthers stepped down on the other side of the buggy before Roddan could move there and offer a hand. She was up the steps and in the office before he followed and joined her.

"I know that man out there," Ann said crisply. "His name is Cultus. He was on the stagecoach which carried me to Mesilla."

Damn Cultus and his misleading report from Mexico. Roddan was sweating. The glittering and successful plan was crashing around him; a fortune was slipping away. Worse, he'd been caught in a mammoth theft! When the story spread through the Territory. . . .

"What is Cultus doing here?" Ann demanded. "And why are you occupying my house? You are, of course. I can see it."

Roddan was thinking in desperate flashes. Where was Geoffrey Carruthers, the brother? Why wasn't he here? Why was the girl talking about "my" ranch, "my" house? Still desperately, Roddan grasped at a dim suspicion forming far back in his mind. He said, "I was sorry to hear of your brother's death."

Her reply was instinctive. "How did you hear?"

Roddan wanted to shout with relief. So the brother

was dead? It didn't matter where, or how. There was just this girl left. This one girl, here alone. He forced sympathy into his expression.

"I have ways of knowing." Now he knew what to say, because he'd been prepared to say it to others, when necessary. "I suppose you know of the money your brother borrowed from me, secured by his interest in this ranch?"

"I don't know any such thing because it never happened," Ann said coolly. "All of our financial arrangements were made between London and Santa Fe banks."

"Obviously you don't believe me, ma'am, and have no intention of honoring your brother's arrangements."

"Why should I pretend to believe something I know is not true? And can prove is not true."

Roddan was sweating again because, mentally, he had stepped to the brink of the final abyss. He knew well what happened in the West to a man who molested a woman. Yet this angry, scornful girl, who'd been simple enough to admit that her brother was dead, was the only barrier between gaining or losing an immense ranch. And if she went free now, she would ruin Simon Roddan for what he had tried to do.

"I've no doubt you'll try to prove it," Roddan agreed. He closed the office door, and they were alone in the thick-walled adobe house.

Chapter Twenty-Three

Hardisty was riding guard when he decided to cut through the last of the rough Porcupine ridges and ride into town to see if the two girls had arrived from Las Vegas. Ann owned a small adobe house on the edge of Canimongo where she and her brother had lived when they had first started to open up the wild reaches of the immense Spanish Grant. He had scouted the house on his way in. It had been ignored, evidently, by Roddan and the new crew.

Canimongo was a small, three-saloon town, quiet in the hot hours of mid-afternoon when Hardisty rode to the back of the adobe house. His grin of welcome came when Rosa Lopez stepped out the back door.

"*Señor Gringo. . . .*"

New clothes had obviously been bought in Las Vegas. Rosa's black hair was combed smoothly back and braided, and the two braids hung in front of her shoulders. In the pink-and-white print dress with narrow lace at the collar, Rosa was pretty, still with the look of half-child, half-woman, both versions lush and ripe.

"You like, *Señor* . . . ?"

"I like," Hardisty said in Spanish. "Where is the *Señorita* Carruthers?"

"She rented the buggy and drove to her hacienda."

His frown was instant. "She wasn't to do that yet. How

long ago did she leave?"

"I think three hours. . . ." Rosa was intently watching his face. For an instant, resentment touched her expression, then her smile came, sad, knowing, older-looking. "I am not your woman, am I, *Señor Gringo?*"

"I've told you, Rosa. . . ."

"O, *si*, . . . but I think, maybe. . . ." Rosa lowered her eyelashes and smiled slightly. "You don't care I see one good-looking Mexican boy at the livery barn . . . ?"

Hardisty had to chuckle. "So quick?"

"I am getting old, *Señor Gringo.* . . ."

"Good-bye, old woman," Hardisty said, grinning as he reined away, and Rosa's parting smile was assurance that she was anticipating the days ahead.

That was Hardisty's last smile as he headed back on the ranch road, looking expectantly for the livery buggy. As mile after mile dropped back and the buggy did not appear, apprehension began to tighten inside. Ann shouldn't have made this abrupt trip to the ranch alone.

The sun was sliding toward the high crests of the mountains off there in the west. In a final blaze, wiped quickly away, the dazzling sun disk dropped out of sight beyond the Reds, and gray-blue twilight began to deepen over the rolling, juniper-dotted landscape. And still no buggy.

This was trouble, Hardisty suspected now, and he wasn't ready for it. O'Meara had been sent to a branding camp at least ten miles from the house. Hardisty had neglected to ask Rosa Lopez if Zeke Winn had come to Canimongo with the girls. The old man might still be in Las Vegas, or wandering in the high, wild country to the west. No help there. No help from O'Meara tonight. There was still a chance the buggy would appear.

The shadows deepened from violet to purple to black. A last glow of rosy light touched high, thin clouds. That faded. Night moved in with brightening starlight thinning the full blackness.

Hardisty walked his horse quietly to the house, which was dark save for a lamp glowing behind shades in the back corner room that was the office. A two-horse team and buggy stood at the short hitch-rail behind the house.

Hardisty tied his horse beside the buggy. He rolled a cigarette, flicked a match alight, and held the dying flame so he could see the buggy seat in the wan starlight. The seat was empty save for a woman's black reticule left carelessly there, and that was enough. The ranch yard was deserted. Only one bunkhouse had lamplight inside. The house was quiet as Hardisty checked his revolver.

He listened, looking around for a moment. If this was the showdown which was due sooner or later, he wanted the odds as even as possible. Finally he drew deeply on the cigarette, stepped on it, walked to the office, mounted the three steps lightly, and rapped on the door.

From inside came, "Who is it?"

"Hardisty."

He heard movement. When the door opened, Roddan's demand was topped with a scowl. "Why didn't you go on to the branding camp with the others?"

"No one told me to. I just got in."

"Move out then, over on Lower Frio Creek, where the other men went. I want all that part of the ranch cleaned up fast."

"I've got a message from the livery stable in town for a lady who's here."

"No lady's here!" Roddan snapped shortly. He was asking, "Where'd you get . . . ?" when Hardisty drew the gun cleanly, swiftly, and cocked it.

"Her buggy's over there. Where is she?"

Hands chest high, open, empty, Roddan backed from

the door as Hardisty stepped in. The man's shell belt and gun were on the desk. He was big, red-faced, handsome, and angry as he looked at Hardisty and the gun.

"Do you see a woman?" Roddan asked.

"I see you. Ten seconds to take me to her. Gamble with the seconds if you feel lucky enough."

Roddan wasted three seconds hesitating. "I'll need the lamp," he said thickly.

"Pick it up. Don't grab for that gun on the desk. I'll be close."

Roddan's big hand went carefully to the glass lamp on the desk. He walked out of the office slowly, back into the house, carrying the lamp, asking over his shoulder, "I take it you're a friend of the lady?"

"You take it right."

"And you rode here and asked for a job to help her?"

"You can answer that now."

Roddan turned into a dark room, speaking again over his shoulder. "Well, here she is, unharmed, even if her feelings have been ruffled."

The lamp, held high, showed Ann on a bed against the wall, a towel around her face, wrists tied behind. Her eyes were blinking in the lamplight. Words she was trying to utter were muffled behind the towel.

Hardisty stepped to the side of the bed. "Put the lamp down. Untie her!"

"Just as you say," Roddan assented.

The start of a smile was starting to spread on his face when the room seemed to explode. Hardisty was not even aware that he was collapsing beside the bed.

He was jolted and jostled, each movement sending sledging pain through his throbbing head. Hardisty wanted to groan, to protest. Instead he kept his eyes closed and tried to sort out the flashes of memory rolling around inside his skull.

He remembered where he had been. On the Vuelta Ranch. Then in tumbling succession came memories of the anxious ride from town, talking with Simon Roddan, the sight of Ann Carruthers helpless on the bed . . . and oblivion. No need to wonder what had happened. His head pains shouted that. Someone else had been in the bedroom shadows, at one side of the door. Roddan had known it when he had carried the lamp out of the office. And Ann, helpless on the bed, had known it and had tried to warn him through the muffling towel. No wonder her eyes had looked wide and desperate. She had been watching the man move noiselessly in while Roddan held the lamp and waited. But now. . . .

What he was hearing were horses trotting, and the creak and sway and jolt of a buggy. Ann's buggy, of course. He was on the buggy seat, and his arms were tied behind him and his ankles were lashed together. Cool night air was against his face. Fragrant hair was against his cheek and in his memories. He would never make a mistake there, Hardisty thought, steadying. He opened his eyes, and the night was around him, wanly luminous with starlight. The sky, completely cloudless now, seemed one blaze of coldly bright stars, with the Milky Way a luminous band still brighter. And it was Ann beside him. His head had been lolling on her shoulder.

He heard her sharp, indrawn breath when he moved, and he asked thickly, "What's happening?" Ann, he realized before his eyes opened, was not in command of the buggy. His arms and ankles would not have been tied if she were.

Ann said, "I don't know what's happening. We were put into this buggy, helpless. Mr. Roddan is driving us up into the mountains."

224

"Who hit me . . . Cultus?"

"Yes. With his gun barrel. He was trying to find out what happened in Mexico, and how Geoffrey died." Even now, when she said that, the grief moved in strong, unsteadying her voice for an instant, holding her quiet for another brace of moments before she went on, "When you knocked on the office door, he pulled the towel up over my face again and, when he heard you talking, he put out the light and waited."

"Have they hurt you?"

"Only bruises on my arms, holding me."

"Where does this road go?"

"It's the old road from Canimongo, running west through the ranch and across the mountains. Not used very much and in poor condition most of the way. We did some work on it lower down."

Roddan's voice on the other side of Ann was coolly distinct. "So he can talk now?"

"And ask questions," Hardisty said. "For instance, have you heard what happens to men who use violence on women?"

"As a lawyer," Roddan said in the same cool tone, "I've heard most of the penalties in law and outside the law. Have you heard, Hardisty, what happens to men who interfere in great plans?"

"Great plans?" Hardisty repeated. Some of the churning, roiling pain was slacking off in his head. The syrupy weakness in his body was receding as strength slowly crept back. A restrained but malevolent anger was growing against this big, red-faced, handsome lawyer. "The only plan I'm concerned with is stealing a ranch from a woman."

"From a helpless woman." Roddan said it with the broad edge of a sneer. "It will do no harm," he went on after a moment, "to admit that both Miss Carruthers and her brother were presumed dead. The only heirs were in England, and not in a position to take over the ranch."

Hardisty let a greater sneer enter his retort. "It's still attempted theft. How much reputation will you have left when it's known throughout the Territory?"

Ann said, "I have assured him that I have written Judge Bassett at the bank in Santa Fe. I have written to the governor. Nothing but getting off the ranch and pleading a mistake in judgment will stop what is sure to happen."

Tall pines were rising blackly beside the road; the cool bite of altitude was in the night air. Hardisty looked back and saw what his ears had told him would be there: a saddled horse on a lead rope was following the buggy.

And that meant? Good God! The man wouldn't dare! Possibly he would to a stranger like Hardisty. But not to a helpless girl like Ann Carruthers. But he would! That lone saddle horse following the buggy was proof enough. The mountains were drowning in night and starlight as Hardisty lifted his voice.

"Where's that flunky of yours? That Cultus?"

"Back at the ranch keeping an eye on things," Roddan said calmly. "If I'm needed, he'll come for me."

"Where are we going?"

"Ahead."

"Where ahead?"

Ann said, "This old road skirts Jump Rock Canyon, one of the deepest in the mountains here. On the other side, halfway up the canyon, is a tall rock butte, shaped like the crown of a hat. Indians once used the top of the butte for signal fires. It's like a bare rock platform and, when you know where to look, you can see it twenty miles away, at least, out over the lower country. The smoke signals, of course, could be seen much further."

"Jump Rock. Did they jump off, too?"

"There's a romantic story about that, about a young Indian who kidnapped the girl he loved from an enemy tribe and, when they were followed and cornered on top of the butte, they chose to jump into the canyon together."

"Very romantic," Hardisty muttered. He didn't really think so, because the danger they were in was as bad, or worse, and it lacked any romance that Hardisty could see. And it was foolish to think differently. Not with this Simon Roddan the man he was, not with the Vuelta Ranch at stake.

Chapter Twenty-Four

The narrow road with ruts seldom used, had been washed, eroded by freezes, melting snow and torrential summer storms so that the buggy lurched constantly, jolting over bared rocks and washed out chuckholes. And when the horses slowed suddenly and halted, the spectral branches of a wind-blown tree were blocking the road. Two days ago, Hardisty remembered, a thunderstorm had growled and exploded and ripped vivid streams of lightning in this part of the mountains.

Roddan muttered under his breath as he stepped out of the buggy. He draped the reins over the off horse and walked ahead and off the road in the dim starlight, seeking a way around the tree.

Hardisty strained violently at the cords binding his wrists behind him. "If I could get a hand free, we'd have a chance!" he said past his teeth.

"I . . . I understand." Ann's voices was strained. She abruptly stiffened. "I just remembered. You're sitting on my reticule, aren't you?"

"I guess so."

"I want it!"

She had turned her back, her wrists and hands tied behind her groping down the seat. Hardisty eased forward.

Ann sucked breath with relief. "I have it!"

"Something inside?"

"A small pair of sewing scissors!"

"Good God! I wouldn't have thought of such luck! Can you get 'em? And cut these rawhide strings around my wrists?"

"I'm trying. There's sewing and a clutter of everything inside and . . . and I can't use my hands very well behind me like this."

He could feel her hands fumbling desperately, groping inside. A stick snapped underfoot and Roddan swore audibly as he explored the brush to the left of the fallen tree.

"Any luck?" Hardisty asked under his breath.

"I can feel the scissors down under everything."

"He's coming back! Don't let him guess what's going on! Here. Get close to me, with your hands against the back of the seat."

"I've one finger hooked in the handle!"

"I'll turn a little, so you can slip the blade down between my wrists and cut at the rawhide. But easy. If you strain and make much movement, he'll suspect."

Roddan had the reins again, and they stopped talking as he stepped back into the buggy. Without comment he turned the horses off the road, up the slight, jolting slope, through brush which scraped and slapped as they crowded through. The buggy lurched; one wheel rode high over an obstruction; the saddled horse behind them blew, snorted as a bent sapling scraped underneath the buggy and sprang upright again. And Hardisty felt chill steel touch his bare wrist.

Ann's back was partly turned toward Hardisty. His back was slightly toward her. Only the darkness and jolting buggy made it possible to sit like this without notice, with the thin hope of helping themselves.

He could feel Ann desperately trying to maneuver the scissors with one hand, keep them open, slide one point under the tough rawhide which lashed his wrists together. If they had been alone, in daylight, or alone under the cover of dark, Ann could have done it in moments. But she was sitting beside the big, hunched figure of Roddan. Moves she made could be felt or sensed. And she had to strain awkwardly, trying to fit the small shears where they would be most effective, then work the blades against the tough rawhide.

The buggy careened back onto the narrow, eroded road and Roddan spoke in a cool, flat voice. "Better, Miss Carruthers, if you'd died in Mexico."

The scissors went motionless. Then their groping, sawing motion started again. Ann's fingers felt cold when they touched the skin of his wrists.

"I'm not sure," Ann said in tight calm, "that I understand you."

"It's not necessary that you understand," Roddan said in the same flat coolness. "But I'll say that years ago I promised myself to become one of the important men of my time. In wealth. In influence. In power. I chose the frontier because competition was less and opportunities for quick success much greater."

Hardisty kept silent. He wanted no action of his to draw Roddan's attention. But Ann, next to the man, evidently felt compelled to say something.

"And now you invite disgrace and ruin."

Roddan was silent for a moment. "I've considered that. Those who plan big often find the risks are big, also. There was risk involved in taking over this ranch, no matter what proof I offered."

"There can be no proof," Ann said flatly.

"Enough proof if you're dead, as was supposed. The

misfortune — the one thing I'd not counted on — was your reappearance this way. And I might even have made terms of some kind with you if this man, Hardisty, had not pulled his gun and admitted he was working with you. That made it necessary that you both die."

The left front buggy wheel rode up over a rock with a violent lurch, throwing them off balance. The scissors slipped out of place. One sharp point gouged into Hardisty's wrist. The right wrist. He could feel the warm blood trickle. Was it spurting? Was it an artery?

"Both of us die?" Ann's voice was thin and strained.

"I'd planned on the fact that you were already dead. When you are dead, the plan will be as good as ever."

The man's greed for money, for power, had unbalanced him, Hardisty decided. They weren't dealing with a sane man now. He swore silently at himself for allowing Ann to get into this dangerous situation. She could have gone on to Santa Fe and safety. Perhaps she could have handled Roddan from Santa Fe. After all, there was law of a sort in New Mexico Territory. But he had believed that O'Meara, himself and, perhaps, old Zeke Winn, once inside Roddan's guard and armed ranch crew, could match the man in callous ruthlessness.

Ann couldn't have guessed how she was upsetting all those plans when she drove to the ranch house too soon. And what had happened was this dilemma they were now in. From the moment they'd been put into the buggy, death had again been moving with them. Yet it still might be possible to reach Roddan. Hardisty decided to try it.

"You're a bad lawyer and a reckless fool if you mean that," Hardisty said coldly. "Other people know that Miss Carruthers is back safe and is the rightful owner of this ranch. Harming her will only snap a trap you won't be able to escape or talk your way out of. Not in court or out of court!"

"I may be reckless," Roddan said evenly, "but I'm not a fool. I'll have nothing to do with this. The road skirts Jump Rock Canyon. In many places a buggy can slip over if carelessly driven. It will mean quite a climb down into the canyon to cut the ties from your wrists and ankles but, when you're found in a few days or weeks, the only blame will be put on yourselves for careless driving."

Hating the man with cold ferocity now, Hardisty still had grudging awareness that Roddan had picked the one way which might be totally successful. It would be judged an accidental death while driving through the wilder parts of the huge ranch. There would be no witnesses. No way, really, to connect Roddan with it.

"I do regret the necessity," Roddan said. "Which is why I said it would have been better if Miss Carruthers had died in Mexico."

Hardisty said through clenched teeth, "The hell with your regrets!"

Words were not going to change Roddan. Nothing he could say, Hardisty knew, would change the man. But he was keeping Roddan's attention occupied while Ann was doing her desperate best to hack through the rawhide strands with the small, pitifully inadequate scissors. He could feel her hand trembling with the intensity of her effort.

"How deep is this canyon?" Hardisty asked.

Ann said unsteadily, "Over five hundred feet."

"Straight down?"

"It might as well be if the buggy w-went over."

"He'll get out with the reins and the lead rope of the horse, and whip the buggy team over the edge, and stand there laughing."

"Please!" Ann begged unsteadily.

"We have to face it."

"Do we h-have to talk about it?" Ann asked almost hysterically.

"Let him keep his mind on that, and nothing else."

He was not sure Ann realized what he was trying to do. Roddan was driving in silence, occupied with his own thoughts, which Hardisty's words might be stirring.

The road ruts had been skirting what seemed to be a shoulder of the mountain. Abruptly on Hardisty's side of the buggy, trees and brush fell away. Yawning space dropped into dizzying depths. In the thin starlight, the opposite side of the canyon lifted sheer and high and black. As near as Hardisty could tell, the road now was running along a narrow shelf, some of it natural, some of it partly excavated from the side of the mountain. There was not much grade.

"Jump Rock Canyon?"

"Y-yes."

Hardisty peered down into the dark depths dropping away only a few feet from the side of the buggy. No one hurtling into space from the rough, narrow road would have a chance of surviving. Horses which shied easily, a driver growing reckless, could send the buggy toppling over the crumbling road edge. One could take the bridle bits and back buggy and horses over the edge, and who could say that carelessness in turning the buggy back had not happened?

Hardisty felt it before Ann did, the give as a strand of rawhide finally parted. He moved his wrists with savage effort. Ann's fingers slipped down, felt the cut rawhide, and began to unwrap the strands. Suddenly his wrists were free! His right hand closed on the small scissors still hooked on Ann's thumb.

"Weakening now," he said as calmly as possible, "won't change his mind."

"I know." Ann leaned out a little, shielding him as she spoke to the silent driver. "If I give my word, Mr. Roddan, that a business agreement between us will be kept, will you listen to reason?"

Bending no more than he had to, Hardisty reached down with the scissors. With only hands free, he still had small chance against the revolver Roddan wore under his coat. But if hands and feet were free. . . .

Roddan's reply to Ann held strain. Cold-blooded as the man was, Hardisty guessed, Roddan was still having to nerve himself to this grisly business.

"Promises made under the circumstances are worthless," Roddan said flatly. "I'm going to have it all."

"And two deaths on your conscience?"

"I have no. . . ." Roddan leaned forward suddenly, peering over past Ann. His left arm swept her back on the seat so he could see Hardisty clearly in the starlight. "Your hands! What are . . . ?"

Roddan grabbed the reins with his left hand and caught under his coat with the right hand. Hardisty thought he felt the top rawhide strand around his ankles separate between the scissor blades but could not look. He had perhaps two seconds left and one chance only. Feet were helpless but he now had two hands, and his lunging sprawl carried him across Ann's lap. His shoulder drove into Roddan's side and hands reached for the gun Roddan was yanking from under his coat. He caught a blurred glimpse of the gun coming out. His left hand slid off the thrusting barrel and his right hand clamped on the gun wrist as the muzzle swiveled toward him.

The wicked lick of yellow muzzle flame, the crashing shot were close. So close that Hardisty felt the wallop of the bullet on his side. And when the second spurt of flame and roaring report came, the convulsive shove of his right hand was pushing the gun muzzle farther out from his body.

The second bullet missed him. And the forward surge of the buggy drove his shoulder harder into Roddan. Wild lurches of the buggy threw them both helplessly about on the seat.

Dizzily Hardisty realized what was happening. The blasting gunshots had panicked the horses, started them running. Roddan's left hand had let go of the reins. His left fist was beating wildly at Hardisty's head.

Hardisty had both hands on the gun now. He had to tear it away from Roddan's grip or be shot again. And one more bullet would end it.

Roddan's left hand stopped striking him and clawed at Hardisty's hands, trying to wrench them away from the gun. The buggy was rocking violently as the two terrified horses raced wildly into the blackness.

Hardisty thought fleetingly of the black depths only inches away from the outside wheels in some moments. The buggy was skidding, bouncing over rocks and potholes in the road. A kind of wild mockery flashed through Hardisty's mind. Roddan had wanted the driver to appear reckless before the buggy finally pitched over into space. And what could be more reckless than this? What more certain to carry the buggy skidding over the road edge and down, down. One turn — it didn't have to be too sharp a turn — looming out of the blackness ahead would be enough to send buggy and passengers hurtling off into the canyon depths.

Hardisty's weight had slid from Ann's lap as she was jolted and tossed toward the outer edge of the seat. Her wrists were still lashed behind, ankles still tied. She was unable even to brace herself against the wild pitching of the buggy.

Hardisty's feet were shoving against the dash, pushing him hard against Roddan while they fought for possession of the gun. Roddan was a big man, a strong man, but he lacked the sheer, cold ferocity that had built up in Hardisty. Nor had his body been toughened by endless labor on the huge water wheels of the Delgado hacienda. With both hands fiercely gripping, Hardisty slowly bent the gun muzzle up and out, away from him.

The pain in his left side came in hot, livid flashes. He could feel blood oozing under his shirt on that side. And the desperate knowledge was in him that all three of them were close to death. But if he didn't stop Roddan fast, he and Ann were surely dead.

The crushing twist of his hands bent the gun back and back. He heard Roddan's gulping groan of effort and, suddenly, the gun twisted out of the man's grip and Hardisty hurled it out into the night.

Now he had only a man on the pitching, tossing buggy seat, a man he could get his hands on without fear of another bullet, a man he could slug with close, jolting blows which smashed Roddan's face, sank into his throat, jolted his jaw.

Hardisty never knew when the cut rawhide around his ankles unwound and fell off. He was aware that the last blow into Roddan's cording throat had set the man off into strangling, coughing gasps. With frantic effort, braced against the back of the seat, Roddan clawed, shoved Hardisty back.

It was then as he came to his feet, to meet Roddan's lunge off the seat, that Hardisty realized his ankles were also free. He braced against Roddan's gasping surge. They staggered, reeled in the rocking buggy. Roddan was trying to shove him back over the dash, down between the horses.

He ducked and spread his feet, and struck up violently into the man's throat again. He felt Roddan staggering, and hit him again, and realized that the man was falling back away from him.

Roddan's strangled cry was not loud. One moment he was looming there, the next he had wilted back out of the buggy. A careening jolt followed as the rear wheel passed over part of him and Hardisty lurched around dizzily for the reins.

They had slipped down between the running horses. His actions were mechanical. Without thinking what might happen, he stepped over the dash to the thin buggy pole, clutching harness on the off horse, and dragged himself forward and clawed up on that horse. Reaching forward from there he got part of the reins and dragged them all up, and reined the frightened team to a walk, then a halt. Roddan's saddle horse halted snorting and blowing behind the buggy.

Hardisty slipped to the ground with the reins and stood sucking great breaths and trying not to be sick. The three blowing horses and his own violent breathing were the only sounds.

"Ann?"

"Y-yes."

"All right?"

"Y-yes! You?"

"I guess so."

Hardisty listened. There was no sound back along the road. He got back into the buggy, slipped his arm through the looped reins, and struck a match. The small sewing scissors lay at their feet. Ann was still shaking when he cut the bonds and freed her wrists and ankles.

"I'll be back in a few minutes. If you hear shooting, and I don't call to you right after, start driving west across the mountains on this old road and get to Las Vegas and Santa Fe. Understand?"

Ann said in a stifled voice, "There's been enough already! Come with me now, while you're safe!"

"And leave Roddan holding your ranch?"

"If it means killing . . . if it means you're going to die. . . ."

"His risk, too. This is the time to get him. I don't think he'll be able to find that revolver in the dark. And his carbine is in the boot on his saddle."

"Suppose he does find the revolver?"

"I'll have the carbine."

"I . . . I can't stop you, can I?"

"No."

"Please, be careful."

Hardisty walked, making himself less a target than he'd be on Roddan's horse. Blood was drying on his wrist where the scissors had gouged in. He hadn't mentioned the wound on his left side to Ann. Now he explored with his fingertips, wincing as he pressed. There seemed to be a bullet groove, a fractured or broken rib, but no bullet deeply inside, with the resultant internal bleeding.

He walked quietly on the inside of the road, finger on the carbine trigger, straining to see ahead, stopping often to listen. Starlight pale on Roddan's face made discovering the man no abrupt surprise. He lay on his back in the road, arms out and, appearing unwounded, he might have dozed off drunkenly in that position.

"Roddan!"

Hardisty struck a match and cupped it over the face. When the match burned out, he felt for a pulse, a heartbeat. And then slowly walked back to the buggy, calling,

"It's me!" as he approached.

Ann, standing beside the buggy, holding the reins, said, "I saw the match. Is he hurt?"

"His horse — that he brought to ride back on alone — did it. Stepped on him, crushed the side of his head."

"If I said I was sorry," Ann confessed after a moment, "I wouldn't be exactly truthful. What will we do about his men?"

"Pay is all they want. They'll scatter as soon as it stops. Even Cultus. Roddan was the only one who had a chance at taking your ranch. It's all yours now, without worry."

"I had a promise," Ann said, "that you'd stay with me."

"Only if you wanted it."

"You know what I want," Ann said softly.

T.T. Flynn was born Thomas Theodore Flynn, Jr., in Indianapolis, Indiana. He was the author of over a hundred Western short novels for such leading pulp magazines as Street and Smith's *Western Story Magazine*, Popular Publications' *Dime Western*, and Dell's *Zane Grey's Western Magazine*. His short novel "Hell's Half Acre" appeared in the issue which launched *Star Western* in 1933. He moved to New Mexico with his wife Helen and spent much of his time living in a trailer while on the road exploring the vast terrain of the American West. His descriptions of the land are always detailed, but he used them not only for local color but also to reflect the heightening of emotional distress among the characters within a story. Following the Second World War, Flynn turned his attention to the book-length Western novel and in this form also produced work that has proven imperishable. Five of these novels first appeared as original paperbacks, most notably THE MAN FROM LARAMIE which was featured as a serial in *The Saturday Evening Post* and subsequently made into a memorable motion picture directed by Anthony Mann and starring James Stewart. TWO FACES WEST, which deals with the problems of identity and reality, served as the basis for a television series. He was highly innovative and inventive and in later novels, such as RIDING HIGH, concentrated on deeper psychological issues as the source for conflict, rather than more elemental motives like greed. He was so meticulous about his research that he once spent days to determine the exact year that blue- (as opposed to red-) checked tablecloths were introduced because all anachronism was anathema to him. Flynn is at his best in stories which combine mystery — not surprisingly, he also wrote detective fiction — , suspense, and action in an artful balance. The world in which his characters live is often a comedy of errors in which the first step in any direction frequently can, and does, lead to ever deepening complications. NIGHT OF THE COMANCHE MOON was the last novel he wrote. He made little effort to publish it and, instead, wrote on the title page, "my last story." His last may very well have been his finest.